Franny, the Queen of Provincetown

Franny, the Queen

LITTLE SISTER'S CLASSICS

# of Provincetown

JOHN PRESTON

ARSENAL PULP PRESS
Vancouver

FRANNY, THE QUEEN OF PROVINCETOWN
Copyright © 1983, 1995 by the estate of John Preston
Preface and introduction copyright © 2005 by the authors
First Arsenal Pulp Press edition: 2005

ARSENAL PULP PRESS
341 Water Street, Suite 200
Vancouver, BC
Canada V6B 1B8
arsenalpulp.com

The publisher gratefully acknowledges the support of the Canada Council for the Arts and the British Columbia Arts Council for its publishing program, and the Government of Canada through the Book Publishing Industry Development Program for its publishing activities.

Little Sister's Classics series editor: Mark Macdonald
Editors for the press: Robert Ballantyne and Brian Lam
Text and cover design: Shyla Seller
Little Sister's Classics logo design: Hermant Gohil
Photograph of John Preston by Mayne Studio

Printed and bound in Canada

> *This is a work of fiction. Any resemblance of characters to persons either living or deceased is purely coincidental.*
>
> *Efforts have been made to locate copyright holders of source material wherever possible. The publisher welcomes hearing from any copyright holders of material used in this book who have not been contacted.*

Library and Archives Canada Cataloguing in Publication:

Preston, John
    Franny, the queen of Provincetown / John Preston ; with an introduction by Michael Lowenthal.

(Little Sister's Classics)
First published: Boston : Alyson, 1983.
ISBN 1-55152-190-3

    I. Title. II. Series.

PS3566.R412F73 2005   813'.54   C2005-903851-9

ISBN-13 1-55152-190-9

Contents

Preface

In 1993, Vancouver's Little Sister's Book & Art Emporium was preparing for what would eventually become the longest and most influential obscenity trial in Canadian history, and author John Preston was preparing to testify in our defense. Preston's erotic novels and stories in gay men's magazines dealt largely with the SM community and as such he was no stranger to censorship at the Canadian border. Canada Customs routinely banned his work from entering the country and he was targeted *as an author* by their fumbling attempts to prevent literature from causing "harm" to Canadians.

Trials move slowly through the Canadian court system, and Preston's life ended before he could testify. His passing resonated among those working on the bookstore's behalf. Here was another talented and charismatic gay author succumbing to the effects of AIDS, one among so many in a generation of silenced voices. Unable to defend his own imagination against a stifling bureaucracy, Preston won the solidarity of authors Sarah Schulman and Nino Ricci, who came to testify on his behalf when the trial began in the fall of 1994, producing some of the court case's most memorable testimony.

Suitably, then, and with tremendous pride, we bring to this series John Preston's surprising and delightful *Franny, the Queen of Provincetown*, a novel about taking care of one's own, and about defiant love, courage, and pride. This edition includes an introduction from acclaimed author Michael Lowenthal, for whom Preston was a mentor, and is further enhanced by supplemental archival material and an insightful essay by Preston chronicler Dusk Peterson. It also includes an epilogue by the author and a working draft of a sequel originally published in the 1995 St. Martin's Press edition.

In addition to its wistful storytelling and dazzling cast of characters, this novel offers an intimate glimpse at the sheer, unabashed humanity of its author. This edition is a tribute not just to the legacy of John Preston, but to that piece of our cultural heritage that, due to AIDS, censorship, and oppression, we may never know.

– Mark Macdonald, 2005

Introduction

Franny, the Queen of Provincetown, John Preston once told me, was his "fuck you to the gay literary world."

To those who remember Preston as one of the key players in the gay book boom of the 1980s and 1990s, this might seem a peculiar statement. Here was a man who published more than forty books, among them some of the best-selling and most talked-about gay-themed titles of that time, from the cult classic porn novels *Mr. Benson* and *I Once Had a Master* to the landmark anthologies of gay men's memoir *Hometowns* and *A Member of the Family*; here was a man who wrote a regular column for the gay book review journal *Lambda Book Report*; who was invited to deliver the keynote address at OutWrite, the national gay and lesbian writers' conference; who made himself a seemingly ubiquitous presence at gay bookstores and awards banquets and in the pages of nearly every gay magazine and newspaper in the country. In many people's minds, John Preston personified the gay literary world. Why, then, would he feel the need to thumb his nose – or flip the bird – at the community that honored him as a sort of fairy godfather?

Preston's defiance (defensiveness?) and the way it inspired the series of monologues that comprise *Franny* becomes understandable in light of his unusual trajectory toward the writer's life. Preston was raised in a lower-middle-class family in the rural town of Medfield, Massachusetts, from which he ventured, during his teen years in the late 1950s and early 1960s, to nearby Boston. There, from men in hotels and at the Greyhound bus station, he was initiated into an underground gay life that was, of necessity, startlingly diverse and devoid of pretension. Soon after, he discovered Provincetown, the resort community at the tip of Cape Cod, where he was rapt by the stories he heard: tales, he recalled in an essay titled "The Importance of Telling Our Stories," "about the horrors that gay life could mean back then, being harassed and evicted, all the cruelty that society could hand out to its unwanted. But there were also proposals about how to change things … voices that had broken the silence and told me about a world of possibilities."

Preston scoured magazines and books for depictions of the gay life he had discovered, and found precious few. When he left for college – at Lake Forest, a preppy private school near Chicago – he harbored intentions of filling that void with stories of his own making. His professors promptly disabused him of those dreams. As he explained in a 1993 speech at Harvard: "I [was] told in college that I wasn't the right kind of person to be an English major, I was too working class and spoke with too harsh an accent." This undergraduate encounter with elitism caused Preston, quite literally, to lose his natural voice. "I spent my freshman year in my room learning how to talk 'right,'" he once wrote. "Eventually I began to sound like a slightly affected voice on public television, not like a boy who had grown up in a small New England town."

After college, having abandoned any writerly aspirations, Preston embarked on what he called his "Grand Tour of the Gay Capitals." He studied sexual health at the University of Minnesota, and, in 1969, helped to found Minneapolis's Gay House, one of the country's first gay community centers. He subsequently lived in Philadelphia, New York, Los Angeles, and San Francisco, where he worked sometimes as a hustler; he was reveling in – and helping to create – the burgeoning post-Stonewall gay community. Preston's activism won him a position as editor of *The Advocate*, already at that time the largest gay news magazine in America. He had achieved prominence in the gay writing world, but as a consumer and a shaper, not, as he termed it, an "originator" of the writing itself.

Energized by his grassroots experiences, Preston eventually did, after moving to New York around 1978, try his hand at writing. The medium he chose reflected his commitment to a particular vision for the gay community (predicated on a kind of egalitarian authenticity) as well as his continuing self-doubt about his potential as a writer: he wrote porn stories for *Drummer* magazine. (As he said in the Harvard speech, "I felt I wasn't entitled to write the good stuff.") Assuming, as did the magazine's editors, that "no one would want his real name attached to such filth," Preston published his first works under a pen name, Jack Prescott.

Although he wrote them precisely because he assumed he couldn't be a "real writer," Preston's porn stories – serialized chapters of what would eventually become *Mr. Benson* – attracted a fervent following among gay men. As the serialization gained in popularity, Preston dropped the pseudonym and began publishing under his own name. He was a writer at last.

This all occurred at the same astonishing cultural moment that is generally viewed as the birth of post-Stonewall gay literature in America. The closing two years of the 1970s saw the publication of Andrew Holleran's *Dancer from the Dance*, Edmund White's *Nocturnes for the King of Naples*, Felice Picano's *The Lure*, George Whitmore's *The Confessions of Danny Slocum*, and Larry Kramer's *Faggots*. These writers (excluding Kramer) – along with Robert Ferro, Michael Grumley, and Christopher Cox – would soon form the Violet Quill Club, dedicated to the unapologetic exploration of gay themes in literature; they were artistic colleagues and a formidable clique in the Manhattan/Fire Island social set.

In 1979, Preston, flush with his first experience of self-identification as a writer, was naturally excited to mingle with this crowd. Michael Denneny, a pioneering editor of gay books who published many of the Violet Quill writers, remembers that he "took John around and introduced him to everyone, which did not go very well." What Preston encountered – or perceived – was precisely the same kind of elitism that he had faced in college. Many of the future Violet Quill Club crowd had been educated at prestigious writing schools and were fluent in the discourse of High Art; Preston feared they saw him as a hack.

To find this attitude now replicated within his own community – the community that he had helped, via his activism, to nurture – made it all the more painful for Preston to bear. "John thought the Violet Quill folk were snobs," Denneny explained in a talk he gave at Brown University in Providence, at a 1994 memorial conference in honor of Preston, "while they, I think, were intimidated by John's sexual outlaw status, and reacted to his ambition to be a writer as if they were threatened by unfair competition."

When the scholar David Bergman was researching his history of the Violet Quill Club, Preston wrote him a letter that looked back on the conflict in political terms:

> There were so few [gay] people who had access to pub-
> lishing that there was enormous pressure put on those
> few who did to make them represent the community
> as a whole. The VQ people, *so* politically naïve and
> untried, were utterly incapable of doing so. They didn't
> have a clue as to why people were so angry that so
> much of their stuff was placed on Fire Island. To them,
> that *was* gay life; to the people who were their critics....
> Fire Island had nothing to do with the gay life they ex-
> perienced in poor neighborhoods, etc.

Noting a strain of racism in one of the club members' books, and the other club members' defense of this problematic tendency, Preston concluded: "They weren't the voices of the gay community, and that's become more obvious and makes them less interesting now, when those voices are more clearly defined."

Preston's political critique was both heartfelt and well-founded. His negative reaction, though, also stemmed – perhaps in equal measure – from his very personal insecurity and sense of having been jilted by the "gay literary world." (In truth, there were other gay and lesbian "literary worlds" at the time, quite apart from the Violet Quill crowd and more accepting of populist forms of expression. But Preston, as much as he resented them, had bought into the notion – fostered by the Violet Quill members themselves, and somewhat confirmed by the cultural establishment – that they were the true yardstick against which to be measured. Hence the "fuck you" that became the foundation of his career, both philosophically and practically.) To a great extent, he once confessed to me, "what I do and who I am was shaped by the Violet Quill guys … and the violence with which they disdained me and *let me know it!!*"

Beyond the clash of politics and personalities, in Michael Denneny's view, "there was a deeper and more interesting distinction between John and the writers of the Violet Quill, a distinction that goes to the heart of the cultural strategies available to a gay writer at that time." The Violet Quill writers, Denneny argues – first and foremost Edmund White – subscribed to a "Eurocentric cultural strategy [that] exalted culture and literature to a realm of perfection." John Preston, in contrast,

> … found himself drawn to another literary strategy, the underground tradition exemplified by the mass market pornographic novels of Sam Steward, aka Phil Andros, and the works of John Rechy…. Working on the economically hard-pressed fringes of book and magazine publishing, this writing harkened back to the classic British tradition of Grub Street…. Often denigrated as

hacks, these writers were the polar opposite of the European aristocrats....

I think the more interesting and important distinction between these two literary strategies lies in who the ultimate reader is seen to be, whose judgment the writer is aiming for and willing to accept. [Edmund] White, of course, has often said that his ideal reader is an educated and cultured woman of a certain age living in a small Midwestern city; someone, no doubt, who has read the same authors White has, with the same appreciation. And John's ideal reader is obviously a young and horny gay man, one of the boys in the bars.

In 1979, not least to escape the gay literary crowd that had snubbed him, Preston moved to Portland, Maine – back to New England, where the accents were familiar – and it was here that he set about writing what would become his first published book, *Franny, the Queen of Provincetown*.

Given the contours of post-Stonewall gay literature as Preston had encountered it in its nascent form, it's worth noting that he set his own novel in funky, democratic Provincetown, rather than in the exclusive enclave of Fire Island; that he gave primacy to a drag queen (and an unattractive, uncouth, "avocado-shaped" one at that), rather than to macho "clones" or disco bunnies; and that his cast of characters is racially and economically diverse.

Most important, Preston eschewed a flowery or self-conscious prose style in favor of a narrative built entirely of simple, unadorned monologues – voices that unapologetically manifest all the tics of social class and region that, as a college student, he had purged from his own speech. In his epilogue to the original edition, published by Alyson Publications in 1983, Preston wrote: "I have chosen not to embellish the speeches with narrative. These are our stories, this is our heritage, and our sagas have their own substance in their own way. They need no justification nor even explanation."

This statement marks Preston's first clear expression of what would become a dominant theme in his career: the notion that, as he once phrased it in a letter to me, his role was to serve as the "scribe to the community." He acted on this idea not only in his own writing, but in two major projects he later initiated with the imprimatur and funding of the Maine Arts Commission. One project was a series of oral histories (unfortunately never completed) called "The Men of Maine: Gay Life Far from the Fast Track"; the second was a writer-in-residence program at the AIDS Project in Portland, whereby Preston took dictation from dying patients and helped them write letters to the loved ones they would leave behind. ("I have become not the author of the story," he wrote of the latter experience, "but the means for telling the story, the tool used by people to let the world, their families, their friends understand what is going on. This is the best writing I can do in a time of AIDS.") Preston's scribal impulse was also embodied in his eventual work as an anthology editor, when he compiled cogent collections of gay writers' autobiographical essays on a wide variety of topics.

But as Preston's first significant attempt to capture the authentic voices of the gay community – not the fabulous, fast-track world of the cocktail-party crowd, but *his* gay world, the world he'd witnessed and worked in – *Franny* always remained his favorite among his dozens of books. *Franny* was a chip on Preston's shoulder that he proudly dared the gay literati to knock off.

I think his loyalty to the book was in truth a loyalty to its characters, since this is a book whose characters and whose intended audience are effectively one and the same. (In the novel, Franny and Isadora are said to frequent a bar called the Inner Circle, and it's the crowd in a bar of this sort that seems clearly to have comprised Preston's imagined readership: "That bar was the first place that I ever went to that made you feel like a human being. It was magnificent to sit there at a table and be able to talk during the afternoon, to see the boys loving one another and the whole group of us having such a great time.")

The writing of *Franny* was also particularly charged for Preston because he was telling the story, not only of the men he had encountered, but of himself. Here I'd like to quote at length (and occasionally out of order) from a letter he sent me about the novel in June of 1993:

> I often speak out against readers who think that all fiction must be autobiography, which seems to rob the author of creativity. But, truth to tell, the autobiographical urge is what sparks *Franny*. It was my first lover who committed suicide in the YMCA in Cambridge, that story is utterly true. The sweater piece in the opening isn't me, but it is my story. So that passion of feeling the feelings of the characters is there….

> Writing *Franny* was the most emotional writing event of my life. I cried and cried at the typewriter. I will never forget not being able to see the keyboard because of my tears. I put my soul into that book, and I don't mean that lightly…. I can feel the room in an old apartment where I wrote it. I can remember the Selectric typewriter I worked on. I remember the horrible sense of defeat when a friend read an early draft and said, "So what? We've heard it all before." I remember a worse sense of defeat when another friend read another early draft and said I must be trying to create a children's book, because it was so simple. I remember getting outrageously drunk while I read and reread the pages and sobbed – I still sob when I read the death scenes. They are my statement about death.

When I had first moved [to Portland], I brought with me a writer named Jason Klein who hated Portland, the cold, the provincialism, etc. We had about a year of being lovers, then I sent him back to San Francisco to live. We never really broke up, it was a great passion of my life … and we talked about getting back together again later. There was a sense that he hadn't "finished" with the big city gay experience, but I had. He needed to complete that part of his life. Anyway, he died almost immediately after he got back to SF. I didn't know that he played self-asphyxiation games during masturbation, but he did, and he misjudged and killed himself. I was a wreck. Probably because I blamed myself for a short while. I had, after all, sent him back to California. And, always remember, this story about the inability to stop a suicide reverberates with Jay's [Preston's actual first lover].

Anyway, there was a lot of grief about Jason's death in *Franny*, though the young boy who dies early on was not Jason. That really was Jay …

God, it was a terror to write that book.

This terror, however, was offset by Preston's joy at the novel's surprising success. Reviewed favorably throughout the gay press ("The best gay novel of the year" – *The Front Page*; "A novel so good it should be true" – *Philadelphia Gay News*; "Charming and delightful, heart-warming and encouraging" – *The Advocate*), *Franny* was also adapted as a stage play that won the Jane Chambers Memorial Award as one of the best gay plays of the year. Preston was over the moon.

When a lot of people who I respected read it or saw
the play … I was enraptured that they understood that
the first two pages, the sweater scene, was my entire
statement about gay life. It was right there and some
very smart people got it…. They sat around and were
awed by the performance, awed by the words I'd written. *They totally got it!*

It was one of the great victories in my life. It was the
beginning of NYC publishers really taking me seriously as a writer. (I had only been an exotic sex player
to them before.) It's when Denneny, [Bill] Whitehead,
[Bob] Wyatt – the great triad of gay publishing – began to hang out with me and began to introduce me
around – it's really why Whitehead introduced me to
Anne Rice…. She still talks about the way he discussed
Franny as the perfect coming out book….

After it was published, I did feel I was really a writer.
Franny really gave me that self-esteem.

Although the glow of that initial success was still vivid to Preston, he had also grown a great deal as a writer and editor in the
intervening decade, and he was able to express doubts about his ac-
complishment:

Franny causes me enormous frustration. First, because
I love it so much. Second, because it's not better. It
was my first book and I wrote it with the consciousness
that I was writing *a book* and that to do so was going
to change my life…. What bothers me about *Franny*
… I didn't know how to write. I had the stories, I had
the passion, I wanted to get it down, but I had never

really been taught anything about writing. So the
structure is off. I hadn't learned to take sentences seriously. I hadn't learned to read stuff out loud to see how
it sounds. When I read from *Franny* now – which I do
often, I love it so much – I change it as I read it, make
it smoother….

When I received this letter from Preston, I had just finished
reading *Franny* for the first time, and, although I couldn't tell him so,
I agreed with his criticisms of the novel.

I had recently turned twenty-four and was only beginning to try
to become a writer. Preston was exactly twice my age, entering what
would be his final year of life. What had started as a professional association, when I submitted an essay for one of Preston's anthology
projects, had quickly deepened into an intense, enthralling friend-
ship of the closest kind. We wrote scores of letters to each other and
spoke on the phone almost every day, often for close to an hour. We
traded gossip and manuscripts. Preston published my work, and I (in
my capacity as an editor at University Press of New England) published his. Eventually, Preston made our association strangely and
wonderfully formal by proclaiming – privately and publicly – that
he would be my "official mentor." (He made the same pledge to two
other writers: Michael Rowe and Owen Keehnen.) Whatever help I
needed, he would give me. Whatever connections I hoped to make,
he would facilitate. I could never, ever, he made it clear, ask too much
of him.

Preston was surprised – and I think somewhat hurt – when he
learned that, this far into our relationship, I had only just now read
Franny – and only done so in order to be able to give him feedback
on the early pages of his planned sequel. ("I probably assumed that
Franny was the reason you were attracted to me and to my writing,"
he wrote.) In truth, aside from his introductions to various anthologies and the manuscripts he had sent me since we met, I had read

almost none of Preston's writing. His guidance was crucial to me – I counted on him as I counted on nobody else – but this guidance was professional and emotional, not especially literary.

For my literary needs, I had other role models. I had graduated from Dartmouth College with a degree in creative writing, and I was, in many ways, a product of the elitist establishment against whom Preston had staked his career. To the extent that I wanted to read explicitly gay writing, I looked toward the by-then plentiful ranks of writers, like Michael Cunningham and David Leavitt, who addressed gay themes in polished, *New Yorker*-worthy prose. I suppose I was a literary snob.

And so, when I read *Franny* that first time, I was not altogether impressed. The characters and situation moved me, but I found the writing stilted, not always believable as natural speech. The novel struck me, not entirely in a positive way, as quaint.

Why, then, return to the book in 2005 and suggest that a new generation of readers – some of whom weren't even born when the book was published – should meet *Franny*? If the novel is not necessarily a great work in purely literary terms, what lasting value does it possess?

Like all the best books, *Franny* includes within its own text the clues to its significance. Near the end of the novel, Isadora says:

> We useta have some big arguments though – 'bout the youngsters. I thought they was gettin' slack, lettin' down their guard. Life was too soft, too easy for 'em. I feared the fight would leave 'em.

> They had all their clothes an' their muscles and their boyfriends they could hold hands with on the street. I was just worried about 'em gettin' off guard. Franny'd just say, "Oh, Isadora, don't you worry 'bout my boys. They doin' fine."

When I first read *Franny*, I felt – as perhaps did many other readers my age and younger – that I didn't need the book. I believed that I didn't need the book literarily (given the many, more polished, gay-themed alternatives) nor politically (given the relative ease of being openly gay in all aspects of life). I felt, in short, that I – and the gay community – had outgrown the book.

My hunch is that Preston would have understood this response, and might even have been somewhat pleased by it. *Franny* fits within a category of gay books that sought in some ways to create their own obsolescence – and I think this is precisely what makes it anything *but* obsolete, but rather earns it a place in the gay canon. (Preston's Alex Kane novels [1984-1987], which introduced a butch gay working-class hero in an era before actual gay firefighters and police officers served openly, as they do now, were similarly fashioned with the hope of someday seeming obvious, even banal.) If *Franny* doesn't strike us as being quite as brave and fresh as it may have been in 1983, then it serves as a gauge of exactly how far we have come from a time when our literature had to imagine into being the very community it simultaneously hoped to portray.

In his epilogue to the original edition, Preston wrote: "I think of Provincetown as an academy; an institution of education where students apprentice themselves and learn from willing teachers how to be gay." Preston, in writing down the stories he heard in Provincetown, was trying to create a book that would serve future gay generations in a similar manner – a textbook for the academy of gayness. As such, *Franny* retains its importance – indeed, gains in importance – as both art and primary source material, a historical marker we do well to preserve.

Preston once gleefully described for me the sense he had "that you and other men are inhabiting a world that didn't exist when I was your age and that I had something major to do with creating it. It makes me feel like Franny."

The better I got to know him, the more I came to see that this facet of Preston – this "Frannyness" – was the core of his personality. The one-time hustler and legendary S&M top, the notorious pornographer, found no greater pleasure than that which he received from enacting, in his own life, the role of the advice-giving, avocado-shaped Queen of Provincetown.

"The most interesting thing about *Franny*," he wrote me in his 1993 letter about the novel, "is that it's not just autobiographical, but I discovered at some point that it was *anticipatory*. I was anticipating growing older. I wanted to become the character I was writing about. I didn't understand that. I didn't get that I was in my early thirties and realizing that my days as a sex star were coming to an end, so I was trying out new roles for myself."

The Preston who befriended me – who with such insistent generosity assumed the role of official mentor – was a persona invented and yet wholly genuine. The role he played for me and so many others is startlingly prefigured within the novel, in the sequence when Franny gives Jimmy a sketch pad and a set of charcoal pencils, and tells him that his art must come before everything else. Jimmy says, "Franny was making me take myself seriously as an artist and so I was. And, as soon as I did that – took myself seriously – the rest of the people around me did too."

Preston, too, learned to take himself seriously as an artist – and earned the right that others should take him seriously as well. In the decade between the publication of *Franny* and his death, he amassed an increasingly accomplished body of work, making the most of his particular gifts (forthrightness, accessibility) and putting behind him much of the self-doubt that had dogged him earlier.

In his final year, Preston turned to the project he had long dreamed of, and which he now felt qualified to attempt: a sequel to *Franny*, updating the novel into the age of AIDS. He began the project one day while waiting in an airport terminal, scribbling notes on a pad of paper, and when he returned home he typed them up and mailed them to me. I asked him to keep going and to send me every new part he wrote.

The basic idea, as Preston envisioned it, was to follow the story of a young man "who comes to Provincetown to fall in love. He falls in love with someone with AIDS who dies. Franny and Isadora are the witnesses to the whole thing. I don't think it can be the handsome clone who I've already written about, though I'm sure that he dies as well. But he's too hard to be the person the naïf falls in love with." He explained that he had "thought of inserting a journalist, someone who goes around and interviews the characters, someone trying to make sense of the epidemic. But it doesn't grab me. I'm more intrigued with the [young man] character, arriving in Provincetown … who's just coming out, hasn't even had sex, but knows he's gay and doesn't know what it means in the time of AIDS."

Preston, face to face with his own imminent death, found himself interested in "the way the spirituality is seeping out of the material, mainly in Isadora's character. This is a battle of my inner self, of course, and there may just be some powerful stuff that comes out in the arguments between Franny and Isadora over spirituality and activism." He further explained: "Franny and Isadora are personifications of my own split over the epidemic – the angry activist vs. the person trying to find some healing."

As he worked on this last project that was so close to his heart, Preston was riddled again with doubt, but it was the doubt of a proud, professional writer worrying about his craft. "The problem with this writing," he wrote in the cover letter accompanying the first batch of pages, "is the terror that's consuming when one deals with issues with such broad strokes. There's such a danger of becoming banal…. Do you realize what a danger it is for a writer to lean on something like *Amazing Grace*?… It's like being asked to walk the most delicate tight rope." In a subsequent letter, he confessed, "The bathos potential is frightening."

Despite Preston's concerns, and despite the fact that he never had the chance to fully revise these new sections, I find them significantly stronger than the original *Franny*: more convincing, more naturally lyrical and unobtrusively moving. Preston had learned to edit himself more rigorously and to accept stringent criticism.

The heart of Preston's approach was still to listen, to capture the voices of the gay men around him. In this spirit, he asked me and some other young friends to write him letters about our experiences, with the explicit intention of using the letters' specifics (and their cadences) in his *Franny* sequel. He asked two pals in ACT-UP to describe their work with the group, and he asked me to provide a riff about playing the trumpet (which I had done for years), because the character of the young naïf – who shared my name and my exact age – would also be a trumpet player.

I immediately wrote a detailed account of playing the instrument, and Preston responded with the kind of unconditional encouragement that was the hallmark of his mentorship: "Your letter about the trumpet was … breathtaking. It is by far the most passionate and wonderful thing of yours I've ever read…. If I were a better person I would refuse to plagiarize any of it for *Franny, Isadora, & the Angels*, but it's so good I have to do it."

Soon after he wrote these words, Preston became too sick to continue writing, and he did no further work on his sequel. The character of Mike, the young trumpet player, had gotten to speak scarcely a dozen sentences.

I always knew how much I loved and respected Preston as a friend, but only now, rereading *Franny* and feeling the regret of never being able to know what he would have done with my voice, do I recognize how much I also came to love and respect Preston as a writer. In a way, I trusted him to tell my story – to make better use of it – than I myself might have. I am saddened at having lost the

chance to hear my voice transformed by Preston's powerful sensibil-
ity, and much, much more saddened to think of all the other voices
he was robbed of the chance to render on the page – most especially
his own.

Franny, the Queen of Provincetown

Franny (1950)

Jesus, Mary and Joseph!

People say the word _queen_ and expect you to run away and hide. Well, to hell with them. I stopped running away from names more years ago than I want to remember. I can't tell you the exact date, but I sure as hell can tell you what happened.

I was working in a coffee shop downtown after I finished high school. I saw this beautiful pink angora sweater in the window at Jordan's on my way to work one day. I was bound and determined to have it. I thought it was the prettiest thing I had ever seen. Soon as I got the money together I went down and bought it. I loved that sweater so much I couldn't even wait to go home and put it on. I ducked right into the men's room and walked out onto Washington Street with it.

I got as far as the Common – going to the streetcar – and a bunch of little punks started to yell at me. All the words: "Faggot!" "Sissy!" "Queer!" "_Queen!_" I could have died. It was that pink sweater. I knew it! I wanted to rip the thing off myself and hide where no one would ever find me again.

And then I snapped.

I had worked my ass off hustling tips to buy that sweater. What the hell was going on that I was gonna let a bunch of shitheads that couldn't even shave tell me I couldn't wear it? Fuck that shit. So I just put my head up in the air and walked past 'em. I ain't never looked back.

Well, I decided if I was gonna go that far out on a limb I might as well find out who was out there with me. They was there. Plenty of them and it didn't take me long to find 'em. Pretty soon I was running around with a whole pack of queens. We was something else. We'd walk down Boylston giggling and eyeing the men and we must have looked like a big puff ball of a rainbow. There was my pink angora sweater and a lavender one and a tangerine one and a yellow one all in a bunch. What a sight!

Whenever some little asshole made a remark, Isadora – this spade we run with – would snap us into place. "Pay no 'ttention, girl," she'd say to us, "you done *earned* that queen title!" And we'd laugh and laugh. No one could get us down when we was together.

Franny & Jay (1960)

FRANNY:

I spent lot of time with Isadora in those days. I thought she was the most beautiful showgirl in the world. When Isadora put on her drag it was like watching a transformation. She'd get up on a stage and start to sing – none of that lip sync stuff, Isadora sang with her own voice – and you'd swear she was a real woman.

After a while she was earning good money as an entertainer. There was enough call for her specialty act that she could hire me to take care of all her wonderful dresses and to help with the makeup and such. Sweet Mother, didn't we have a blast in those days! We traveled all over the country. It made me so proud to be with Isadora, to know that I had something to do with making the world a prettier place, ya know?

Times were hard then. We didn't know how bad things was till we went on the road and had to go to places like Chicago and little towns like Nashville. Jesus Christ, Boston looked like the Promised Land when you put it next to them.

And that's when I met him. It was in Chicago – we used to play there a lot. Whenever we hit the city we'd always go to the Inner Circle on Sunday afternoon. It was the little bar down a half flight of stairs stuck way outta the way on the North Side.

Isadora would play one of the big drag bars near the Loop on a Saturday night. We'd sleep in and then, round two or three in the afternoon, we'd get up and go uptown. Sunday was the day, ya see. Any other time you went into that place it would be dead as a bar could be, but Sunday afternoon the Inner Circle would fill up. There'd be me and Isadora in our finest drag, and bikers, and hustlers and any kind of queer in the world there was at that bar on Sunday afternoon. I swear to God it was the biggest gay party in North America.

I used to like it 'cause it was so clean and nice a place. It wasn't one of them sewers you had to spend time at – all smelling of piss and stale beer with no signs out front and windows painted black so no one had to look in and see us standing there. And it wasn't like where Isadora would play where there'd be all these tourists gawking at you. That bar was the first place that I ever went to that made you feel like a human being. It was magnificent to sit there at a table and be able to talk during the afternoon, to see the boys loving one another and the whole group of us having such a great time.

But this one afternoon when Isadora and I went to the Inner Circle we had to stop short at the corner of Lincoln and West Armitage, just about where that bar was. We had to stop 'cause there was this sight that terrified even us.

To this day I don't know why it happened. I suppose someone didn't pay off somebody or something. But that entire block of West Armitage was lined with police cars. On both sides. They just sat there without any sirens going, but they had those blue lights swiveling on top of 'em. It looked so horrible, those moving lights turning round and round and not making any noise at all.

There was cops standing outside each one of the cars. They had billy clubs in their hands, just waiting for one of us to make a move. There was a crowd that started to build up. But we were a pretty pitiful group. Not one of us – not even those big, mean bikers – was going to be stupid enough to walk down that block.

Mind you, there wasn't ever a doubt what they was doing. They was closing down the Inner Circle. They didn't want that queer bar to mess up the neighborhood anymore, I guess. And we knew we were going to give in. Or at least we thought we was. I was so sad to think that the only place in the whole goddamn country where you could sit and drink a decent drink and not feel like you was one of the scum of the earth was going to pass away.

Then I saw him. He was standing over to the side a little bit, across the street from me. He had on these clean-cut clothes. He wasn't no Harvard boy, but he looked good and respectable.

Well, he might have looked like a college boy, but I swear to God you could tell there was something going on there. The fists on his arms was clenched tight as a construction worker's. He was shaking, just shaking with anger at those cops standing between him and that bar.

JAY:

I had just come from my parents in Glencoe. They'd given me a hard time and I just wanted to get away. The doctors had taught me that much … to leave when something was too stressful. I had a hard time with stress. I got sick and had to spend some time in a hospital. I wasn't insane or something, but I got sick and had to have medical attention.

That's what my mother called it: medical attention. She didn't want anyone to think there was anything wrong with her son. So I didn't have a breakdown. She said I got *sick*. My father never called it anything at all.

The hospital wasn't bad. They gave me medicine so I didn't get upset as much as I did before. They talked to me a lot. I talked to a shrink; I talked to my therapy group; I talked to my recreation group. But they were just words, words, words. If I ever said anything to anyone that really meant anything, they'd shut up as tight as my mother and father.

The people in the hospital always used to say, "Trust us, Jay, we're here to help you. You have to trust us to get better." But whenever I wanted to talk about being queer, they'd become steely cold. They'd close down on me and leave me alone with my words, leave me alone with my shame for ever speaking them.

God, I was so scared. I used to have these horrible dreams with demons coming to devour me. I could hardly sleep from the fear of those things. All the doctors did was increase my medication.

I finally decided I had to get out of there. I learned quickly enough how to do it. All you had to do to be "better" was to make believe nothing was wrong with you. They'd never really know the difference if you didn't tell them.

So I stopped trusting my shrink and didn't mention thinking about men anymore. I started spending a lot of time with this one girl so they'd think I was normal and while I still had my nightmares, I didn't tell anyone about them. I kept them to myself.

I got to go home. I had learned some things. Like walking away from stress and not revealing all the things that were on my mind. I controlled everything so I wouldn't bother anybody.

But they took away my medication when I went back to Glencoe. If you're not sick, you don't need medicine, they said.

Without my pills I had to see too much. All my senses were open. I didn't have any filters left to keep things out. Things like the silence whenever I walked into a room. The way people would look at me. The sad expression on my mother's face. The hurt looks my father gave me when he didn't think I was looking back at him. The way my classmates would avoid me in the hallways at school.

They were so silent because I was strange. They were frightened that I'd go crazy on them if they talked about anything real or important. They were scared I was going to be berserk on them and start saying crazy things.

So they kept quiet. They just looked and smiled.

If they had yelled at me or cursed me or given me some argument or called me queer or *anything*, it would have been better than the feeling of shame that came over me when everyone was so quiet. If I was so confused when nobody said anything to me, then it must've been all inside my head, I used to think. It must've been my fault. It must've because I was sick.

I started to feel as though I wasn't any good. Like it wasn't worthwhile living. I spent every week sitting in my room and smoking dope, waiting for Sunday when I could go to the Inner Circle and be with people who made me feel better. I could sit and listen to them laugh. I could always find a man who'd hold me in his arms and let me touch him. No one would touch me except for the men at the Inner Circle. The rest of them were all so frightened because I had been sick. They knew what was really wrong. But they would never talk about it and they would never hold me when I was frightened. It was as though they thought they'd catch it from me or something.

They all thought that they could just sit quietly in the house with me and wait it out. They never said so, but I knew they were praying I'd just pass through this phase and stop being queer. It was just a *transition*. I was just going to go through it. Hell, no one was going to help me until I was finished with my *transition*.

When I walked to the head of the block and saw all those police cars, I suddenly felt as though the whole world made sense. For the first time in years there was some reason, some force, some thing standing there that made me understand. I had something to fight against for the first time.

There were police cars. There were policemen. Finally someone had the guts to tell me to go to hell instead of playing all the games and making me more confused with silence. They were real demons, not the imaginary ones. They were daring me to do something with a directness that challenged me, instead of all those whispers and sly looks that people always used to use. Franny was right when he told me I was shaking. I was shaking with this determination that I had never even known existed within me. It was as though I was a locomotive building up steam … getting ready for the big push. Here it was. This was my chance to say no to somebody. You won't do it to me anymore.

My body just moved up West Armitage on its own power. I could feel every muscle in me – tight as metal. I stared right in the eyes of each and every one of those cops as I walked by them. I almost wished they'd have tried something. I wish they had laid a hand on me!

FRANNY:

Isadora and me just couldn't believe that this kid was walking in the middle of all those cops. This little college kid. She said to me, "Well, girl, you goin' to let that child walk up there all alone?" And next thing I knew, there went the most beautiful drag in America, proud as a peacock, walking up the street behind that young guy. Isadora nearly fooled those cops for a while. I mean, Isadora's drag's so good it'd fool almost anybody. But that girl couldn't hold it in. She walked fast enough to catch up with the boy and took his arm. She kissed him on the cheek and laughed out loud. Then the two of them walked down the stairs into the Inner Circle with big grins on their faces.

One by one the rest of us followed. Oh, good God alive, we were a parade. It was like the end of something. Just like when I had that pink angora sweater. There are just times when you gotta walk by and hold your head up and keep on going. If you do it, you won't ever have to look back. But you have to keep that head up, goddamn it.

ISADORA:

Y'all gotta understand this: Franny was the ugliest bitch I ever did lay my eyes on. That queen could put on makeup and all, and her hair could be styled by the best of 'em, but she could only look less ugly when she was finished. Not pretty, just less *ugly*.

I supposed that's why she and that boy got together. Franny didn't have much sex life. There weren't many men back then that'd care about personality or that stuff. They just wanted a pretty piece. That Franny was never gonna be.

But when she walked into that bar that day and found us sittin' at a table, she come over and sat down and I knew there was trouble comin' right then. There was a look about Jay. His eyes had this emptiness all around and there was this funny way they had, jumpin' up an' down, and movin' around. I knew there was just too much sadness in him. Franny didn't see it though.

You gotta understand this too: Franny thought she could make the world pretty if she just had enough time to throw enough rhinestones and glitter. She saw this boy and it was goin' to be easy, she thought. She'd just pretty things up for him and everythin' would be fine.

She adopted him that very day. Might as well have had papers drawn up at the Cook County Courthouse. He was part of our tourin' group next thing I knew. I shoulda said somethin'. I shoulda stopped it. But Franny had someone to love for the first time in her life. I couldn't take that away from her. I didn't have the guts. But I knew … I knew there are some people the hate's got to too strong. Some people who ain't gonna be saved no matter how much rhinestones and glitter there is in the world. That boy Jay was one of 'em.

FRANNY:

Oh, I tried! Mother of God, how I tried. I thought that anyone who'd be so strong he could walk up that line of police cars in a place like Chicago just had to be strong enough to make it.

I had such plans for him and me. I was going to give him all the things he needed to be happy. We went back to Boston after we finished touring with Isadora. I had a few pennies set aside and I figured he could go to Boston State or somewhere and finish school. And then he'd make a fine lawyer or even a doctor.

I was living in Somerville then, near Sullivan Square. We got him a room at the Cambridge Y so he could have his own place. He'd come over to my house and I'd cook him meals and get him to laugh and we'd talk and talk about everything in the world. He was so delicate. Not like me, I mean he wasn't nelly or anything. He was just so delicate, like something you had to put your arms around and protect.

That strength of his, though, it'd come out sometimes. He was going to these meetings all the time. He'd come back and he'd be all hot and bothered and angry about the world and he'd give me these lectures about politics. They were the best times, when he was pissed off at somebody that'd be doing something like those Chicago cops.

But … when he wasn't mad, he'd start to brood. I'd get worried then. Those eyes of his'd get funny-looking and weird. He'd sit in the corner and just frown. "Go on out," I'd say and give him a couple bucks. "Find yourself a man tonight," I'd tell him. I'd do anything to change him outta that dark mood.

Sometimes it'd help if we walked. We walked all over Cambridge and Somerville that summer. The nights'd be lovely, least that's how I remember them. Soft summer nights, the two of us walking down Mass. Ave. together.

But then there was this one night. He'd already started to take drugs. I never said anything about it to him. It broke my heart to see it happen.

He'd even steal from me. He could've had it all. Jesus, if it'd really helped, he could've had it all. But drugs?

Sometimes they musta made him feel better. Somehow. There'd be times when he'd be all smiles and laughing again. But, it seemed as if each time he stopped laughing the moods got worse and worse. And that one night they were the most terrible they had ever been.

He'd taken to starting to cry for no reason. I'd find him sitting in my apartment and he'd just be weeping his little boy heart out. He'd done it that night.

When I walked him to the Y near Central Square, I had this horrible feeling. It was the most horrible feeling I've ever known. All I could do was to look at him and tell him just one thing: "I love you more than I love my own life." I already knew it wasn't enough.

The next morning he wouldn't answer his phone. That wasn't like him. I called every half hour to wake him up. After noon, I knew. I called the manager of the Y and all I said to him was: "There's a dead boy in Room 365." I sat there in my living room, my body just cold feeling and I waited. Then I called back and found out the truth. My Jay was dead. My strong little man Jay was dead by his own hand and it felt as if my whole world had collapsed down on top of me.

ISADORA:

I found Franny a couple days later. She wouldn't answer the phone and she kept missin' shows down at the club I was playin'. I knew somethin' bad must be up.

I went over to her place and knocked on the door. There wasn't no answer, but the door weren't locked either. So I went up in. There was sittin' the most miserable-lookin' queen that God ever thought up.

She was in the livin' room. Pale as a Canadian ghost. Lookin' at pictures of Jay and just sort of starin', mumblin' 'bout razor blades and sleepin' pills. I got the news outta her. I wasn't surprised. But I was worried 'bout Franny. Worried that the same thing was happenin' to her, the same slippin' away outta life.

The one thing I do know is that you gotta stay pissed at the world. Ya gotta stay mad at the people that are pullin' all the shit on you. If you give up, you gone. Franny thought it was her fault. That she had fallen down on that boy. The idea! That Franny didn't love that boy enough!

I knew I hadta get her going. Like when someone's freezin' to death in the cold, you gotta keep him movin' before the blood stops. It's the same thing with hurt. Ya gotta keep the circulation goin' or the hurt'll take over.

So I went down the street to Morrissey's Funeral Parlor on Broadway. Those micks hadn't never seen anything quite like me before. But they know the color of good money. I was headlinin' those days, besides, any queen with a butt as high as mine could always pull in a few more bucks on the side with the old johns that hung 'round the shows. I had plenty to give that boy his funeral. I got my shyster lawyer to do the legal things and I even called Jay's folks when I figured out where they were.

Next day I got Franny together. It didn't seem right to go the funeral home in drag, so I just touched us up a little and dressed us in our street clothes. We walked down to Broadway to the home and went inta the chapel.

No one else showed up. It was just the two of us. The place seemed so empty. I had bought some flowers, but they didn't help – made it worse, in fact. There was this cute Irish priest that Morrissey's had got to come an' say the words.

I couldn't understand some things. They kept the casket closed. Wished I had known they planned to do that. Franny and me would have wanted it open. Fuck tradition. We wanted to see the boy off proper.

The worst part came at the end. I had a big Cadillac hired to take the body to the cemetery. The young priest stopped us and whispered some things into Franny's ear. I didn't hear it, but there was this look come over Franny. A look of such contempt!

FRANNY:
He told me that a suicide couldn't be buried in consecrated ground.

ISADORA:
I found out all 'bout that when we got to the buryin' place. The digger told me that's where they put people ain't baptized or ain't Christian or is suicides. There was this corner with a separate fence. That's where they put Jay, outta the way. All the other stones were just little markers. I got one for Jay that was bigger than almost all them put together. But it was still like he was being shamed once more – all over again – even in his ending.

FRANNY:
All the time we sat in the funeral home chapel I was thinking about my sister's boy, Frank.

He died in Korea, in the war. I remember that funeral and it wasn't like Jay's. There was crowds of people at Frank's funeral at St. Patrick's. They had soldiers in uniform with their guns pointed in the air when you walked in. My sister wailed all through the ceremony; her husband sobbed; all the friends that gathered cried. They made this *noise*. That's the way it should be – should be noise when someone dies. *Loud* noise!

And then we all went out and got drunk enough that the father started to damn God for stealing Frank away from him when he was so young. I was thinking about all that while Isadora and me sat in that quiet, quiet chapel and listened to that idiot of a priest say the words as quickly as he could so he could get out of there fast enough to get in his eighteen holes of golf. But when he told me that about the consecrated ground, I began to burn inside. It was like he lit coals in my heart. I was so pissed off that I thought I was going to sock him.

ISADORA:

I thought Franny'd be that kind of basket case she had been. I was still workin' at bringin' her outta it. So, after we put Jay in the ground, I stopped at a package store and got us a bottle of Chivas. There's nothin' like good Scotch to help a body through a crisis.

Well, we got back to Franny's place, all silent like, and I poured us a drink. Franny took that one, and another and another and the queen was just flyin' high. Next thing I know I'm chasing her up the stairs to the roof of that building she lived in.

Oh, God Almighty, what a show I got to see that night. There was this *mad* queen standin' on the roof of this triple decker in Somerville, Massachusetts and she's standing there with her little fists up in the air like she was punchin' the sky, screaming out loud; she was just yellin' her lungs out.

FRANNY:

If there is a goddamned God up there, I want to tell you something!
You are a goddamned fool and I've had enough of your meanness.

ISADORA:

There was tears runnin' down Franny's cheeks. The little bita mascara I put on for her that day was streamin' down. That queen was too far gone to even know it. She had somethin' to tell God and, by Jesus, she was goin' to say it.

FRANNY:

I want you to take your consecrated ground and I want you to shove it where daylight never goes. My Jay's too good to spend eternity with the likes of you that made him so miserable. You take your cemeteries and you take your priests and don't you ever bother with me again. You are a mean old bastard. You got one too many of my children already and you ain't gonna have any more of them. I am not going to let you take any more of them!

ISADORA:

You ain't seen life if you ain't seen a queen howlin' out her soul and tellin' God to take a flying leap in Somerville, Massachusetts. I want you to know that I was screamin' and yellin' right along with Franny by the time she was done. I was tellin' off God like he was a two-bit pimp tryin' to get inta my money. We just screamed ourselves out that night.

It was right to do that. That Jay was Franny's child as sure as if she had brought him inta the world herself. The parents sure as hell didn't want that boy. I called those granite-assed sons of bitches in Illinois and told 'em about Jay and they just said to me: You bury him, we don't want him back here. Can you imagine a mother not wantin' to bury her own son? If you can, then you can imagine that that Jay had become Franny's own flesh and blood.

Finally, we was just tired out and collapsed on the roof. I put my arms around Franny and she let rip, the sobs heaved in her chest and the cries of a mother mournin' her baby went out in the air over that godforsaken city. I just held on and held on. In my own way I knew that Franny's cryin' meant she was goin' to make it. Those yellins at God were goin' to be her salvation.

Hate has to be shoved away. I know that. Ya gotta fight hate off with anger. If there is a God, and he's Jesus's father, then he has a dumbassed son, that's all I got to say about that turnin' the other cheek shit. Maybe sometimes. But this life is too hard to do that more'n once or twice. There's too much hate to ignore. And the only way to handle it is to scream and yell and fight dirty.

'Cause if you don't, then the hate's goin' to go inside you like a cancer and spread in your own soul an' take away whatever it is that makes you wanta live.

That's what happened to Franny's boy child. He lost that fightin' spirit we saw in Chicago and he let the hate get under his skin. You either send that hate right back out there where it belongs – to crackers or dumbassed micks or stupid cops or whoever – or else it's gonna get to you.

It's gonna kill you.

FRANNY:
I became hard after I lost Jay. I sure as hell was gonna do what I could to make sure there weren't no more Jays in this world.

I was going to go out there and I was going to start acting like it was a matter of life and death that those boys got treated like human beings. They *were* human beings, goddamn it, and I wouldn't let no one tell me otherwise. Specially not my own kind.

Franny & Joel (1963)

JOEL:

Franny and I had gone to Chelsea High School together, way back when. We were the two sissies in that school. We didn't really care; we could always go over to Boston for what we wanted to do. I was called Joelle back in those days. That's what Franny still calls me.

I never lost track of Franny in all the years. Even after I met Michael, my husband – I know I'm not supposed to use that word; it's supposed to be lover, but he _is_ my husband in my mind, like it or not. Michael and I met at Sporter's Bar over at the bottom of Beacon Hill. It was dreary, but it was easy to get to, and besides, I met someone as nice as Michael there so I won't spend any time complaining about it.

We just fell in love and … got married. Not formally, of course. We didn't even think about going to a minister like they do now. But we made our own vows to one another and we've tried to stick to them. He already had a house out in Lynnfield. It just happened naturally that I moved in with him.

Our business was almost a mistake. Michael is very, very butch. He's a welder by trade. He used to work at the Charlestown Naval Shipyard. But one day he saw me doing some designs – I've always been good with designs, you see – and he took them out to the garage and next thing I knew he had put together these pieces of scrap metal he had. They came out just right, according to what I had drawn up.

Well, people started to admire it. So we made some more and

gave them away as Christmas presents one year. Then they seemed so popular – they were things like ship's models made out of iron and brass with very simple, tasteful lines – that we would go to street fairs or down to the beach during the summer and set up a table and sell them.

Before we really knew what had happened, we were in business for ourselves and Michael left his job to work full time in the garage.

He didn't like Franny coming around so much 'cause, well, Franny was so *obvious*. But Franny was my best friend in high school, and I told Michael you can't turn your back on your friends, there are too few of them as it is.

After Michael stopped workin' for the Shipyard and did the designs full-time he relaxed a little about things like that. But he still worried about the neighbors and what they'd think when Franny would come by.

Anyway … after a while our business got so big that Michael needed a helper. We put an ad in the *Globe* to hire an apprentice welder. It just so happened that Franny was sitting in my living room when the first person came over to apply.

When Jim walked in I nearly had a heart attack, and I knew that Michael was even more upset than I was. Jim had good experience, he had callused hands of a hard worker and he seemed to know welding. He looked all right in most ways, but he had this earring on. A pierced earring. And he … well, was just so *gay*. What more can I tell you. There was that earring and the way he talked and all.

Well, Michael wasn't about to have a little faggot in the business, or so he said after the kid had left his name and address and gone home. I thought that Franny was going to jump across that room and strangle my husband in front of my own eyes when he heard that.

The two of them screamed and screamed at one another. Franny said some hateful, hateful things.

FRANNY:

I can't believe you closet queens. Who the hell do you think you're joking? There you sit in this little town in the suburbs. Two men living together. You think people don't know? Your house is full of tchotchkes and all the frilly little things that Joelle loves so much. Who is being fooled when they walk into the middle of this mess? No one! But you're going to turn a beautiful gay boy away from a decent job as though you're saving something by doing it!

You have no right! You have no right to turn him away. Don't you know what's going to happen to him? He's going to go out there into the city and he's going to get cold. That smile on his face is going to get bitter and hard. He's going to remember you and all the others like you and he's going to turn away until he's alone. And that's going to do him in – that's loneliness.

You're so proud you have one another. You two, together in secret in Lynnfield. No one knows, you think. You think you can send that boy back to make his own way 'cause *you* did it. Hell, you ain't done shit but grab hold of one another out of fear. You're two scared queens afraid of your own shadows.

You have no right to make that boy go through what happened to us. You are no better for all those tears and all those names they called you all those times you've been so frightened. You are not better; you're scarred. You have no right to turn around and leave a scar of your own on one more person to make it even. Not on someone as young and full of trust and hope as him.

JOEL:

So there they were, fighting and yelling at one another. Michael saying that it was one thing for Franny to talk, living in the city and all, and another one for us two to have to live in Lynnfield, where there was no privacy. And all of a sudden I started to weep.

Michael was shocked. We certainly had had our little spats before. But he had never seen me cry. Isn't that funny? I mean, the way queens are supposed to be and how we actually are can be different. I didn't used to cry at all. Maybe it was holding in all those things and trying to fool all those people in Lynnfield for Michael's sake. I don't know.

The two of them stopped arguing and pretty soon Michael walked around the table and put his arm around my shoulder and asked what was wrong. I told him.

Franny was making me remember the pain we used to have when we would go and try to get a job. When people would snicker behind our backs as we left off our own applications. When they never gave you a reason for not hiring you, but you saw the ads in the newspapers for days and days afterwards, the job was still open.

Franny was right. If *we* wouldn't hire that young man because he wore an earring and maybe looked a little gay, then who would?

There we were, two men in our thirties. We owned our own company, so who *cared* what people thought? Besides, we lived together in our own house and everyone in town really did know what it meant that we spent our vacations in San Francisco and that we had those beautiful poodles I walked every day through the center of town. We were trying to make believe we were invisible. But, I told Michael, we're not. You can't be invisible when you got a queen like me sharing your bed with you. It's a cruel deception to think no one knew that.

Well, Michael is a good man, better than Franny knew. He thought for a little and then he stood up and he went and picked up the phone and called that kid right back that afternoon. Gave him the job.

Jim, that first young man we hired, turned out to be the best worker we ever had. Him and Michael even go out and do all kinds of butch things together – things *I* would never do with Michael – ski and climb mountains.

Pretty soon we had call for even more work, and it was just natural to ask Jim if he knew someone who could weld and would like a job. His eyes lit up and he said, "Sure." So, this is, oh, two years after he started to work for us and him and Michael had become such buddies, pals, so Michael just automatically said, "Well, bring him over on Monday and he can start right away." We trusted Jim totally, you see. He'd stay in our house when we traveled and take care of the dogs and plants for us. And he did some of the business banking for us and everything, so it seemed perfectly natural to have a friend of his work for us too. We thought they'd be happier with someone they knew working beside them.

The only problem was … his friend was a woman. On Monday morning the toughest, smallest, butchest dyke I ever saw drove her Vespa scooter into our driveway and stormed up to the garage that was still where they worked. Good Lord, she even had a leather jacket on and was smoking a cigarette – I wouldn't even smoke a cigarette in public, it's so … improper.

Michael just stared at Valerie, that's what Jim called her. But what could he say? Well, I was all ready for hell to break to loose that night when the two kids left for the day. I could just imagine Michael bellowing about a dyke being in the shop. But, when he walked into the kitchen, he had this big smile on. "You know what?" he said to me. "She's the best welder I ever laid eyes on."

After that, well, there was nothing left. Here were the two of us, once thinking we were respectable members of the Lynnfield community, and now we had a gay boy with a pierced ear and a dyke with a Vespa working for us.

Our business got bigger still. We started selling my designs to the finest gift shops, nice places in Hyannis and even up in Kennebunkport. We landed a big, big contract with a chain of stores out in California. We moved the factory part to a new building near the expressway, we had become quite the industrialists by now.

We hired more people. We just fell into hiring all gay boys and dykes. We're good to the kids and they are good to us. They put in a good day's work for a good day's pay and they know that we're not going to say anything if they wear a T-shirt with printing on it or an earring or anything. What difference does it really make to us?

Those kids keep us young, besides. Michael and Jim have their own special relationship. Jim doesn't know it, but he's going to inherit the whole business when the time comes. That's how much Michael and me think of him.

Franny & Joshua (1966)

FRANNY:

I got tired of touring with Isadora. The travel got to be too much for me. I suppose I was getting old. I wanted to settle down and I decided to move over to Provincetown. There'd be work in the summer, dressing and making up the shows that come to town, and I thought maybe I could even get my own act together and do a couple gigs there.

I was tired. Jay was still with me and carrying him around inside made me weary. I thought it'd be a good change to stay in one place.

So I went and found myself a cute little cottage right on Commercial Street. I could sit in the front and watch the harbor across the way.

JOSHUA:

Franny caused a stir when he moved to P-town. Sure, we were all used to drags. But they were entertainers. Even if they were outrageous on the street, we could look at them and make believe they were just carrying over their act from the night before.

Other men dressed like women, too, of course. Even regular townspeople, but only on Halloween or New Year's or for a special party. But Franny was different. He was just out there – a queen of the first order no matter what he wore. And worse: He was planning to live in town the whole year 'round.

I think Franny would have looked like a queen if you dressed him in full leather. It's the way he walks, his little mannerisms and his utter unwillingness to try to change them or to hide them that gave him away.

FRANNY:

I knew I wasn't the most popular person with the year-rounders. But I just said to hell with it whenever one of them would pull something on me. Hell, if I couldn't live in Provincetown, I wasn't going to be able to live anywhere.

Besides, I was having my own good time. Mainly, I used to go to the Madeira Room at the old Pilgrim House, where all the shows'd be. The showpeople knew one of their own kind so I got some work. And after I did my job backstage, I'd go and sit at my own special table and find some boys to talk to.

I'd either go to work on the ones that needed me, or I'd sit and enjoy the ones that were okay on their own. I suppose they would sit and talk with me 'cause I was some kind of curiosity. They did love my stories about the old drag shows though. And about the old days in general. I don't care why they talked to me, I just cared that they did. They was so young and there was so much that was going to happen to 'em and I just wanted to be a witness. I didn't want to rule their fucking lives, I just wanted to watch 'em grow up.

And if the respectable citizens of Provincetown didn't like it – they could kiss my ass.

JOSHUA:

The gay guys in town – even the women – tried to ignore Franny that first year. He'd never got invited to anyone's house or to any parties. He'd go to the various bars at night and sit by himself and just watch. I guess some of the kids who'd come over to P-town thought he was interesting, there always seemed to be a group of them sitting with him.

I wouldn't have talked to Franny myself if I hadn't seen the way the other year-rounders treated him. It never would have occurred to me that we'd have anything in common.

But I hadn't moved to Provincetown to stay in the closet. I had left a good job – a very good job – and my family and friends in Minnesota and made the trek to Cape Cod because I wanted to change my life. It boils down to one simple thing. I wanted to be gay. Not just trick on weekends and not just hang around bars. I wanted to be able to forget that there was anything special about loving men. I wanted to live someplace where it could be taken for granted. Strange, when it's put that way. I say I wanted to be gay, but then I say what I really wanted was to forget about it.

I knew what I had to do was to get everything in proportion. I had to learn to like myself. I had to learn to accept who I was, what I was. If all those people were so upset about this one person living in their midst, then it meant that they were repelled, not by Franny, but by something in themselves. I decided I had better find that part of me that was Franny and learn to love it as much as I was starting to like the rest of my package.

If I was half as butch as I thought I was, then why should I have to avoid being seen with a queen? The same goes for the rest of the guys. If they were so masculine, then why did they have to shy away from spending time with someone who was nelly?

Don't misunderstand me. I wasn't playing any hero. But I decided that someone in town should make Franny feel at home. Or else this place wasn't the perfect refuge I thought it was. And if it was going to be my job, I decided that I was going to do it right.

I made a point of sitting with Franny just a little bit every once in a while at first. I'd always find an excuse to talk and trade news and gossip on the street if I ran across him during the day.

Pretty soon Franny started to feel more comfortable with me. I realized that I put him off as much as he put off the rest of the people. But we relaxed with one another. He started to come over to my guesthouse every morning for a cup of coffee.

It became part of my daily ritual. He used to arrive with his own mug of coffee in the beginning. I finally asked him, "Franny, why don't you just drink mine? I have plenty made every morning." He looked over to the huge urn I used to make coffee for all the guests who'd come down in the morning and he lifted his eyebrow and said, "Joshua, how can you expect a queen to drink that cow's urine. For God's sake, you *percolate* it!"

That's Franny, blunt and direct and always making sure that everyone knows that he expects the best out of life, whether it be coffee or friends or whatever.

Franny's like an institution for me now. The very few times he's left Provincetown for a trip it's really thrown me off. I almost don't know how to start my day without him coming around for his morning cup of coffee and to trade stories about the night before or the dirt on the newest arrivals at my house or the latest star in the bars.

Not the least present I've gotten from him over the years is the special coffee pot he finally gave me at the end of that first summer. It's just for the two of us. And now I look at that big electric percolator that the guests drink from and while I sip my freshly ground French Roast that's been brewed in the Melitta, I *do* wonder how they drink that cow's urine.

Franny & Ted (1967)

TED:

While I was going to Northeastern I used to go over to Provincetown every chance I could get. I was working in Boston in the summers for my tuition, so I never had anything but weekends free. But every Friday I'd drive down the Cape to P-town.

It was like a magic place to me then. I would drive across the town line and I'd just feel freedom coming over me. I could camp, I could trick, I could hold hands with a man, I could do anything I wanted to without worrying about what people were going to say. Best of all, I could dance.

Do you realize you couldn't dance with another man in Boston then? I'm talking about not even fifteen years ago. Can you believe it? I spend so much time in discos now that it doesn't seem possible that dancing could ever have been banned, but it was.

That first summer I was in P-town we used to be able to dance at the Back Room at the Crown and Anchor. They never played any slow songs – only fast tunes so you wouldn't have an excuse to touch the guy you were with. But at least it was dancing.

FRANNY:

Oh, how I loved to watch you! Joshua, big and butch as he is, would sit with me and I'd sip my cocktail while he pulled on his Budweiser and we'd watch you youngsters move out on the floor so fast and smooth and agile. You was gorgeous out there. I could've spent every night just watching you if I had the energy. But just the looking at you would make me tired!

There was some kind of release going on with that dancing that I had never known. I don't think even he had known it before that summer. But by August even butch Joshua was up there on the platform shaking his rear end with the best of 'em. I just knew it was a good thing.

TED:

Then on Friday night I got to P-town. I was just getting off work after a long day, but I still went to the Back Room about ten, early, but usually there would already be someone there to cut out with on the dance floor. The bouncer stopped me at the door, I think his name was Terry. He pointed at two state cops that were standing on the edge of the room and warned me that they were there to arrest anyone who danced with another man. It was against the liquor laws.

I was furious! Women were getting raped in the city and old ladies were getting robbed in the middle of the Public Garden and they didn't have anything better to do than come to Provincetown and make sure us *fags* stayed in our place. But what the hell was I going to do?

FRANNY:

Joshua and I got to the Back Room and saw those cops. I started to burn. I went over and held the acid off my tongue, but I asked them just what did they think they were here for?

"Just enforcing the law, *sir*." They said it real nasty to me. Joshua was pulling at my sleeve and trying to keep me out of trouble. He dragged me over to our table and he let me sit there and fume while he got our drinks.

There was Ted – probably the most handsome of 'em all – standing over in the corner. I had seen him over and over again, every Friday and Saturday night. He was the very best dancer in the whole town. I used to think he was so good he should have gone into show business. He could kick his legs as high as any chorus girl in Las Vegas and he'd do these cute things with his behind, wiggling it real sexy life, but always in perfect time to the music.

He was getting chased around by everyone that looked at a pair of pants that season. I wasn't interested in that. I was interested in him because I saw that same spark that Jay had when he was at his best. A kinda defiance. You could see the way he looked at straight people. It was different. If he could tell someone was straight, he didn't give a good goddamn about 'em. That boy had spunk and fire in him. And he kept it all for the right people. Smiling at gays and scowling at straights.

While I was looking at him, Joshua came back with my cocktail. Joshua doesn't have that anger in him, it's something more calm. More concrete too, maybe. But what Joshua and Ted had in common was that they wasn't going to let no one push 'em around. Joshua wasn't going to make a big deal out of it, but he made it clear as day that he wasn't putting up with this stuff. And the boy wasn't neither.

I looked over at the two state troopers and I stared at them so hard they looked away from me. Then I waved Ted over to our table. I used my best stage presence to appear normal to Joshua and sent him off to buy the boy a drink. Then I asked Ted, "Do you want to let them get away with this?"

TED:
So there I am sitting with this funny-looking queen with a round body that looked like an oversized avocado. And he's asking me, Are you going to take it sitting down? I couldn't imagine what he had in mind, but I just answered that I couldn't go to jail. I had to finish school. "If I did something to make sure you weren't arrested, would you come here tomorrow night and dance with my friend here?" I looked at the hunk Franny was talking about as he brought back the

drink for me and I guess I giggled. Hell, I would have danced with him any time!

JOSHUA:

Here I had spent the whole summer telling myself that I had made a new and decent friend out of Franny. I had lulled myself into thinking that all of the fears that the others had were just illusions. But when I saw the look on their faces when I got back to the table, I knew I was in for trouble.

I tried to convince myself that Franny was just trying to fix me up with Ted. But there was so much more mischief in his eyes that I knew it was more than that.

When I sat down Franny just asked me: Will you dance tomorrow if I do something to make it legal? I got a lump in my throat and started to think of arguments. But what the hell. I came to Provincetown to stop running away from things. This was no place to change that program.

TED:

I still thought that queen was crazy. But I was good to my word. I showed up on Saturday night right at ten o'clock when the music started to get going good. Humpy Josh was there sitting at the table with Franny. I went over and we had a drink. I looked and saw the two state troopers. The same ones as the night before. I swallowed my drink down and told Josh: Now or never. We got up on the platform and started to dance with each other.

But there was someone else on the floor too. Franny had hired this girl to stand in the middle of the room all by herself and just do some kind of solo number. When the troopers, big red-faced men ready to bust fag heads, came over to us, they had to ask me, "Who are you dancing with?" And I just pointed to the girl out there by herself on the middle of the floor. "She's my date." Josh said, "Mine, too."

The troopers looked at us with their jaws open. There wasn't a thing they could do. If we said we were dancing with the girl – and they figured out that the girl would back us up – then we weren't dancing with each other and they couldn't possibly stop us.

They both got all huffed up and I thought for a second they were going to do something. But instead they stormed out of that bar and onto Commercial Street as though they were Custer trying to get out of the Last Stand.

It was a wonderful night. As soon as they left, the whole bar climbed up onto the stage and started to dance with us. Everyone was dancing together, and laughing and tasting one of the sweetest victories we'd ever imagined possible.

Franny just sat at his table on the edge of the room with a big shit-eating grin on his face.

FRANNY:
I knew then that my boys wouldn't have to stop dancing ever again. It was the way it was supposed to be.

Franny (1969)

ISADORA:

I useta always have a two-week gig in P-town during the summer. I'd visit Franny and have a good time talkin' and goin' over the old days.

This one day I was down at the Portuguese Bakery eatin' my roll an' coffee and readin' the *Globe* when I got to this story. I couldn't believe my eyes. Holy Shit! A buncha queens down in New York had gone *crazy*. Some cops tried to break inta their bar and scare 'em and they just said: "*NO!*" Next thing, they was throwing things in the air and chasin' cops down the street with their spike heels, settin' fire to cruisers and causin' all kinds of havoc.

Well, I mighta thought it was funny, but afta I raced back to Franny's I found her sittin' in her kitchen at her pink Formica table with a look on her face. A expression of violence that no queen ever wore was in front of me. She looked up at me and I could see she already had the paper in her hand open to that same story.

FRANNY:

I should've been there! I should've been there!

ISADORA:

Let me tell you: It's a good thing that queen was stuck two hundred and fifty miles up Cape Cod. Otherwise there'd be some NYPD blue-coated pigs six feet under. That queen wouldn't ever have just bust ass if she'd'a been in Greenwich Village. That queen woulda done murder.

I am glad I ain't never seen that look on her face again. The anger is healthy. But there was murder to be done if she had a chance that night.

FRANNY:

That day in June is branded in my brain. I knew as soon as I read that paper that there was other queens in the world that was doing my work too. We wasn't alone. I knew it then. There was others.

JOSHUA:

I think Franny expected a full-scale revolution to break out that day. I didn't understand why it was so important to him. He came over to my house and sat in the sitting room. All he could say was: "The queens have finally started to fight."

FRANNY:

There are times when you just know the rules've been changed. There wasn't anything immediate going to happen. Shit, I had already waited more than half my life. I certainly was willing to wait a few more years. 'Cause things had to be different now.

Franny & the Professor (1975)

LEONARD:

I was a pitiful drunk in those days. I can't even remember when I originally met Franny. I must have been totally inebriated. I know I blacked out. The first time I *remembered* seeing him was the next morning. I was sprawled out on his couch. The sunlight in Provincetown was so bright it always hurt my eyes when I opened them after a drunk.

There used to be a checklist I went through upon waking up in my drinking days. I went through my routine:

Had I thrown up? A quick glance at my clothed body showed no evidence of regurgitation.

Had I been robbed? My wallet seemed secure in my pocket so that was not a concern.

And finally, where do I get another drink? I very carefully lifted myself to a standing position. I slowly walked towards what I presumed was the kitchen. There I was greeted by the figure of Franny sitting at his table drenched in that appalling sunlight. He wore an enormous caftan over his full figure. It was a Hawaiian print with colors as dreadfully bright as the sun.

I never did get a chance to inquire after that bit of the hair of the dog that bit me. Instead, I received a lecture like none other I had ever heard before.

FRANNY:

My father was a boozehound too. So don't try and pull any of your lies with me. I know all the tricks and all the excuses. If you want a cup of coffee I'll give you one – a cup of the best in town. But you can go to hell if you think I'm going to give an old sot like you a drink in my house.

You winos is all the same. You probably don't even know what you said to me last night, the things you told me. Just like my old man, hiding behind your bottle.

So I'll save you some embarrassment and I'll tell you what you told me – as least that much that made any sense … what you told me before your slurring got too bad for me to understand you.

You cried on my shoulder about the bad life you had. How sad and tragic you made it out to be! How miserable you said it was! You old drunk. You are in misery 'cause you want to be. You love your life and all the excuses you got for drowning your sorrows in alcohol.

Well, I ain't got time for that shit. I woulda just passed you by if that's all you had to say for yourself. There are boys out there dying in alleys and getting beat up in school and they haven't given up. By what right do you?

You know what I see when I look at you? I see a pitiful, sick old man who's trapped himself. You blame the world for your sadness, but you done it to yourself. You are so typical. There ain't nothing special about you. You're just like a whole bunch of idiots, doing the same thing.

You come to Provincetown every summer and get drunk on the very first day, dontcha? You get drunk and kill your sense and get up enough courage to go out and suck cock. Isn't that so? If you're lucky, you'll be drunk enough you won't have to remember it the next day.

Then, when the end of the season comes, you go back to your fancy college where no one'd dream that the *great* professor would ever put a prick in *his* mouth. And you just sorta sip your fancy wine all day, hoping that you won't never have too much to make you do anything you'd regret.

Maybe you need to go down to New York once in a while and get yourself a hotel room and a bottle and a hustler. That'd help you for a while, wouldn't it?

Well, I don't give a damn about your good name and I'd just as soon piss on your college as anything else. *But I want that goddamn book!*

I have hundreds – thousands – of boys out there waiting to read something good about themselves. You can pickle your liver after it's done for all I care. But you gotta write it, professor, you gotta finish it. It's more important than you are. You can't flush something like that down no booze toilet.

LEONARD:
My book.

I truly must have been smashed to have brought that up. The manuscript was decades old. I had written it in the flush of a first love in my undergraduate days at Princeton.

It was a silly tale. The projection of the wonders that I had thought would lie waiting for me and Scott Tanner, my roommate. We were going to be different. We were going to have the love affair of the century with high adventure and glamorous living in Paris, Rome, Madrid … until he married that hateful cow to secure his parents' approval – and her money.

And what of me? I was meant to forget Scott and our dreams and go on. A liaison between friends? Male friends? How *British* of us to do that in our Princeton days, Scott said. How very amusing. How very indiscreet of me to bring up such a delicate matter.

My pain was salved by work for a while. At least long enough to allow me to earn my doctorate. But, later, among all those college students … so many of them would remind me of Scott … I found the warm blanket of alcohol to cover myself with. It left me alone with the good memories and blocked the painful recollections.

When I was drunk I could imagine that any of the faceless bodies I'd find – or buy – were Scott.

Franny was right. I was a pitiful old sot. I had romanticized everything to keep myself from that reality. But the sour taste in my mouth, the raspy feeling of my two days' growth of beard and the rank odor of my unwashed body were all suddenly, unavoidably, illuminated by his harsh words. My past was not a cherished moment of visionary love; it was a sordid chapter in an old man's pathetic self-destruction.

ISADORA:

Well, Jesus Christ. Next year I go to P-town like always and Franny's married! That girl's more'n half way through her time on this planet and she's gone and got her a husband.

I swear to God, I walked up to that cottage that first day and there Franny was, sittin' on a rocker in her big tent dress and knittin' socks. As God's my witness, it's true.

An' there's this rumply old fella wanderin' 'bout, Leonard. The Professor, Franny calls him, and tells me he's there for the summer to write his book.

They done took that little spare bedroom and called it a study with a typewriter in it an' all. Holy shit! I said it out loud. "Franny's got herself a man!"

JOSHUA:

They were the perfect couple. From the first day on. I never saw them fight, not once. Franny used to fuss over the Professor a lot, and cook all the meals and clean the house all summer.

The Professor had his own routine. He'd read his newspapers and magazines and journals in the morning, then talk to whoever Franny had invited over for lunch, and then he'd spend the afternoon in his study working on his book. At night, they'd come over and play hearts and whist with me and Ted. Franny would only let us serve lemonade when we were with the Professor. Later on, he'd go to an AA meeting or home to bed and Ted and I would take Franny out so he could watch the guys dance.

Franny still went out almost every night during the season. He couldn't stand the idea of losing contact with everyone – "his boys" he called us. He used to sit at his table – there were maybe a half dozen bars by then and Franny had a special table he'd try to sit at at each one. None of the managers or owners of the bars were embarrassed by him anymore, either. He had become a fixture and was a sure way to make sure a crowd stayed put.

Franny had some favorite things to do in those days. He liked to read all the buttons and the T-shirts. Whenever he saw a new one he'd run across the room and grab whoever was wearing it and talk.

FRANNY:

I'd see a button like ANITA BRYANT SUCKS ORANGES, and I could've died laughing. Sometimes I'd write down a real good one like that so I wouldn't forget to tell the Professor about it in the morning. The idea! Anita Bryant sucks oranges.

All these boys would wear shirts from bars in their home cities so you could see where they were from. I'd run up to 'em and see the name and place. Oh God! I'd get so excited when I'd see a new one. Imagine, there was Minnesota and Washington, DC, and even California boys there. Provincetown had come to be a big melting pot with everyone trading stories and making new friends and dancing with one another.

When I found a boy wearing a college shirt – no matter if it was Yale or some community college – I'd find a way to make sure he was doing okay. If there was any trouble with his grades or anything, I'd invite him to lunch right the next day and the Professor would tell him what to do to make it right. He even gave some of them extra help if they needed it. He was such a wonderful teacher for those boys.

JOSHUA:

During the school year the Professor would go off to Amherst. It never seemed to bother Franny. The Professor would always show up again at Christmas and later for Spring Break. I thought they should just move to one place or the other, but they said they didn't want to. They were happy as they were.

I never took the book seriously. You know how everyone's always writing a book nowadays. Then one Christmas Ted and I went over to Franny's with our presents for them. Franny was just beaming when he handed each of us an identical package. We opened them and there it was: the Professor's book! I had never read such a lovely story about two gay guys before. Ted and I actually read it at the same time. Reading that book together helped us – a lot. It was really a good book. The Professor became a big celebrity in town. And Franny was never happier.

ISADORA:

Joshua's the one that called me in St. Louis. The Lord only knows how he got the number of that backstage pay phone, but he did.

When I heard the news I just ran to my dressing room and changed so quick I forgot and left half my makeup on. I took the first plane to Logan and stood there holdin' my breath while I bought me a ticket on that PBA. I ain't never gone up in one of those tin can things before and hated to do it then. But I didn't have time to drive. That poor queen. Only four, five years o' happiness and the world come down on her again.

I got all shaken up flying all over that water an' the way they nose-dive those toy planes o' theirs into the sand before you can even *see* the landin' strip should be a crime. But I got there an' jumped a cab t' Franny's. I expected it to be like Jay all over. Oh, how could so much sadness come to one person?

Well, I walked into that little house ready for the howlin', expec-tin' a spectacle. But, there was Franny … almost cool. She was lettin'

Joshua and Ted take care of things, serve little drinks to some other people there and such. It seemed so … cool. I couldn't figure it out. Franny came right up to me and hugged me. For a while there I was scared. I thought it was one of those times when people is so bad off they in shock. I said something to Franny about it.

I never expected the words I got from her.

FRANNY:

I can't begrudge God for taking people when it's their time. The Professor stopped his drinking and he wrote his book. That's more'n most people get.

I ain't going to get mad 'cause a good man died after a good life. There's too much more to get mad with to waste all that on something that was allowed to run its natural course.

The Professor, he was like a gift to me. A balancing for the rest of it. And I was a gift to him. Who knows, maybe God was trying to make his peace with me? Who would have thought that rummy of a Professor would turn into a good person like that? But he did, Isadora, he did. He made my life sweet and comfortable – even if only for a little while.

Besides, look at all these people. The Professor ain't going out of this life unnoticed. He's going to have a decent funeral and there's going to be lots of people to honor him. He's going out the way a man should.

I'm even going to let them bury him in the churchyard. He'd of wanted that.

I can't spend my time crying and moaning about this, Isadora. I ain't been robbed this time. There's no cause to spend my days grieving what's gone when there's so much work to do.

This ain't God doing me dirt. This is the end of a full life and I can't begrudge God for having Nature take its course.

JOSHUA:

Ted was the one who cried the most through the funeral. He owed the Professor a lot. He had tutored him through his senior year to get Ted's grade point average high enough for law school and had written a special letter of recommendation that probably secured his place at BC Law. Somehow, all the working together drew them close. Ted was going to get his diploma that June. What really broke him up was that the Professor wouldn't be there to see him graduate.

It was late spring, so a lot of people were back from winter vacations and the church was packed. Everyone had loved the Professor and the place was full of flowers. All of us went to the grave and a whole long line of his friends walked past, each one of us depositing a single shovelful of dirt over the casket.

Franny, of course, came last. He dropped a single white lily and cried very, very softly while the attendants finished filling the hole. Then, when they were done, Franny turned away from the mound and smiled.

Franny & Her Boys (the 1980s)

ISADORA:
That summer the Professor died I decided to retire. I had plenty o'
money and sorta fancied the idea of me being a lady of leisure, sittin'
on a patio and sippin' daiquiris while the men walked by. Old as I was
gettin' to be, they was still plenty o' them eyeing me an' I thought
it was time I stopped runnin' 'round the whole country. It seemed a
good idea to slow down enough to let a few more catch me while they
was still chasin'.

I got me a house in Provincetown too. An' Franny an' me'd
spend summer afternoons together on the balcony o' the Crown an'
Anchor an' she'd drag me down to the Boatslip for tea dance. Summers was nice with Franny.

We useta have some big arguments though – 'bout the youngsters. I thought they was gettin' slack, lettin' down their guard. Life
was too soft, too easy for 'em. I feared the fight would leave 'em.

They had all their clothes an' their muscles and their boyfriends
they could hold hands with on the street. I was just worried about
'em gettin' off guard. Franny'd just say "Oh, Isadora, don't you worry
'bout my boys. They doin' fine."

FRED:
I used to walk past the house at least twice a day going to and from
work. Almost everytime I went by Franny would be sitting up there
on the porch. I used to laugh with my roommates about it. He was
always knitting. So we had nicknamed him Madame LaFarge. The

other thing I noticed was how many different caftans he had. There must have been one for every day of the season – patterns, solid colors, stripes, everything you could think of – all of them in bright colors that caught the sun that reflected off the water. We never talked that first summer. We'd just nod to one another the way you do when you see someone often and they become familiar to you just because of that.

The next year I came back to Provincetown again. The first time Franny saw me that second year was also the first time he spoke to me. He was sitting on his rocker as he always had. He called out and asked me to come up the stairs. I just thought he wanted to say hi and welcome me back to town.

When I got there and stood in front of him he reached out and ran his little hands up and down my legs and then touched my chest. It was a kind of inspection.

"Where did you ever get those muscles?" he asked. "You were skinny as a rail last season."

I giggled with embarrassment and with a little bit of pride admitted that I had been doing some exercises. "I guess I just got tired of being a seventy-pound weakling getting sand kicked in my face all the time."

We chatted a while and then I went on to work. I thought that was the end of it. But the next day he stopped me again and asked me just what exercises I did. I was uncomfortable talking about it, it sounded a little too vain to go through the whole routine with him. But he was insistent and I described the sit-ups, pull-ups, push-ups, running, those kinds of things that I did. He picked up on my discomfort and just laughed more at me: "Why should you ever be upset about making your body pretty?"

The third day I automatically stopped to talk to him. There, beside his rocking chair, was a big cardboard box. "It's a present for you," he said. "Joshua – the guy down the street – has gone and got himself a new fancy set. No reason to let this one go to waste." I opened the container and there was an old, but usable, set of weights. Just a beginner's set, really, but more than I had had. "Anything worth doing is worth doing right," was the end of the conversation.

From then on he'd keep asking me about my progress – how many pounds was I lifting? What was my weight now? Was I eating the right foods? He'd read things in the newspaper about weightlifting and clip them for me – hints and advice types of things. By the end of the season he was even coming over to my house and watching me with my routine, egging me on to keep up the pressure and build my muscles as much as I could humanly do it.

I finally asked him, one day after the first of September when I was getting ready to go back to Boston, why he had taken such a strong interest in something like my weightlifting and bodybuilding when it seemed so far away from anything Franny would normally care about.

FRANNY:
I know you're doing it to feel good and look good. Shit, nothing wrong with that. I think it's wonderful that you attract all those others with your body. But what I really want is for all them straights to see all those muscles on a gay boy. I want 'em to think twice before they pull any shit on one of you. It'd do 'em good to get a little scared of a gay boy for a change.

FRED:
That winter I kept up my program at a gym. I was getting to the point where I was even considering entering into some competitions. One night, it was a cold winter night, I was walking to the Eagle and I had on a big, baggy coat. I was huddled over, fighting the wind, as I walked down the streets of the South End on my way to the bar. Suddenly there was this guy standing in front of me with a knife in his hands. I didn't even think about it, I grabbed his wrist so fast we were both surprised. The knife stopped in midair. My grip is so strong that

I knew, as soon as I got over the shock, that the knife wasn't going to go anywhere so long as I held on to his wrist. I began to squeeze his forearm. The knife clattered down on the ice-covered sidewalk. I just looked in his face. He tried to swat me with his free arm, but I stopped that as easily as the first. He was no match for my strength.

I think I would have just let go once I had disarmed him. But I remembered what Franny had said. I realized that he had only dared to attack me because of the heavy coat that hid just how muscular I was. I also knew that if he had seen someone as defenseless as Franny, he would have mugged him and gone home and crowed to his buddies about the easy marks that were wandering through the South End on their way to the gay bars.

I could never have planned what happened next. It was because of the fury I felt as all of that was going through my mind. I just started to twist his arm, more and more. I got it up behind his back. He begged me to let him go. I forced him down on his knees. Then I kept up the pressure until I heard the unmistakable crack of his elbow joint dislocating. He screamed with pain.

I released him then. There was an expression of disbelief on his face as he looked down at the dangling limb. I told him where the hospital was and started to walk away. I turned back and gave him a final few words: "You go back to your neighborhood and you tell your friends that the queers down on Tremont Street are getting awfully mean these days. It's not a safe place for them to try any games."

TERRY:

I had been going to Provincetown for years. I met Franny and the Professor when I was still in college. I used to go to their house for lunch every once in a while. It was an experience. The Professor would sit and tell great stories about the other faculty members at Amherst, about their foibles and their inflated egos and we could all laugh about our own teachers and see them as human beings instead of the tin gods they tried to be. We'd all sit around and sip iced tea till it was time for the Professor to go into his study and write his mysterious book.

I'd always see Franny in the bars at night, sitting at a corner table watching us. By the end of the summer he knew everyone by name and it was almost a ritual to go over and have at least a short conversation with him every night.

I think I was always … well … special to Franny. I've always been very physical and I would dance myself into a sweaty exhaustion. He liked that. At least he always said he did.

I had thought I had lots of friends in Provincetown. At least everyone had been friendly to me and I never had any trouble fucking. But the summer I came back after my first year in New York a lot of the guys were leery of me. I had taken that intense physicality of mine and found new things I could do with it when I started going to the leather bars down in the Village.

When I returned to the Cape that year I had a new look – a studded belt, engineer boots and a leather jacket. Everyone's initial reaction was to give me a wide berth. I suppose I was too far out for them. It was a shock to everyone but Franny.

FRANNY:

You know, Terry, when I was coming up I was such a queen that it didn't make no difference what I wore, people'd always know what I was. Didn't bother me, except for them other queens in their three-piece suits who'd run away from the sight of me.

Well, I learned soon enough that they didn't really so much think I was horrible and disgusting as they was jealous. Jealous of my freedom to walk around like I wanted to. And jealous of how I could make myself look better'n God meant me to be.

You just ignore those boys. They'll get over their being uptight in time. And then they're going to start coming on to you like you never hoped they would. 'Cause you're acting out their dreams and that's what they want to be doing themselves. They want the freedom to look like you look and act like you act. Maybe a little different, each one in his own way. But it's not different from those queens who used to be scared of me. They're jealous in the same way. Envious of you being willing and able to put on clothes that say who you are, or who you want to be, or whatever.

Now, don't go and get upset at an old queen like me when I say this, but what you got on is drag just as sure as my fanciest ball gown. But that's good. That's being creative and that's making your own way in the world and not letting someone else tell you how you should be. Don't ever lose that, boy. Don't ever lose that ability to take life and change it to what you want it to be.

Wear your leather and show 'em all what a man you are. Show 'em how proud you are of it. It'll do 'em all a world of good. And you mark my words, they're going to start coming round to you soon enough.

You look good, honey. You keep that going if you have any brains in your head.

TERRY:
After that, I learned to love to promenade with Franny. Especially after the bars closed. We'd walk up and down Commercial Street. I'd be in full leather and he'd be in those clothes that might as well have been full drag. The people would look, they'd stare. The gay guys would try to cover their uptightness with some jokes, but Franny and I would ignore them all.

After Franny went home, I'd stand in the street and just watch the men. I figured I'd really done it now. No one was going to want anyone like me, someone who was purposely acting weird and different.

But day by day, week by week, and certainly season by season, things changed. There were more and more leather jackets on Commercial Street. More men who looked like me and who wanted things the way I did. It wasn't so bad after all. In fact, it got to be pretty hot stuff in time. There were so many of us! Gay men who were manly and proud of it. All of us in our leather and flannel and boots and all the rest of it. What a sight we must have been to those straights. A regular goddamn biker brigade right in the middle of Provincetown.

JIMMY:

About the third year I was in Provincetown I began to get worried. I had been on the road the whole time. Cape Cod in summer. Key West or Fort Lauderdale in winter, San Francisco and New York in between time.

It had begun to be a blur. One big disco with a multitude of faces that no longer seemed different from one another. Bodies in sunlight, bodies on dance floors, ups in the morning, downs at night. Sex. Endless mechanical sex.

I was beginning to freak out. I was beginning to stare at the men I saw in all the places I went to in New England and Florida and San Francisco and see the problems they had and think they were going to be mine. I had missed some turn in the road.

No. That's not right. I had taken the right road, but I had gone too far. I was a twenty-five-year-old waiter who lived day to day on his tips, when I got them. I needed more than that.

I had done all this to come out. I had immersed myself in the ghettos to experience as much as I could as quickly as I could. But I was in danger of being swallowed by it.

Of course I knew Franny. Everyone who spent any time in Provincetown did. Usually I just joked around with him though. I never thought that funny-looking drag queen could have so much to say to me.

One day, though, I was sitting on a bench on Commercial Street and Franny came by holding an umbrella to protect himself against the sun. I must have looked miserable because he stopped and sat down beside me and asked what was wrong.

It all just spilled out. Dancing was fine. Provincetown was fine. Being gay was fine. But, I told him, I don't even know where my best friend lives. What does that say? The person I like best in the whole town and I only know him on the dance floor. I didn't even know if I would recognize him if we both weren't at tea dance or in Back Street at night.

Franny just listened quietly. Then he asked me a lot of questions. Where was I from? What had I studied in college? What did I enjoy? Where did I want to be in a few years? I gave him the answers and he nodded.

I had been an art major. Once I had wanted to be an artist. Franny wanted to know about my work. Did I have any he could see? There were some sketches up in a locker in my room. Would I bring them by? To his house? Sure, I said.

Later that day I did drag them out. They were all in a big over-sized portfolio. I took them over to Franny's house and opened up the thing. I hadn't looked at that stuff for over a year.

Franny asked me all kinds of questions about each piece. What medium I had used? What was I trying to say? What had I learned while I was doing it?

Just in the explaining to him I began to look at my work again. I saw some promise in it that I had forgotten, remembered some project that I had hoped to do next, thought of some experiment I had conceived. For the first time in years I began to be interested in work once more.

FRANNY:

It was touch and go. There was this little boy strung out on speed and being lost in the crowd instead of using it. Being led away from life instead of finding his way back into living, the way they're supposed to do in Provincetown.

And he had lost something. Something wasn't there. All I could do was sit and hold my breath, sit and hope I was saying the right things and asking the right questions. What the hell do I know about art?

My Jesus, what was I going to do with this one?

JIMMY:

So that afternoon after I showed my portfolio to Franny, I went over to the Boatslip for tea dance. I was boogeying away with the guys and there's Franny standing on the edge of the floor with a big package wrapped like a Christmas present. He lifted a finger and crooked it to let me know he wanted to talk to me.

I fought my way off the dance floor and found Franny at a table on the patio. "It's for you," he said. I opened it up and there was a sketch pad and a set of charcoal pencils.

"Go home and draw," he said and he left.

It's a moment that's still as clear to me now as it was then. Do it and come back to the dancing when you have time. But go do it first. Work. Your art. That had to come first. I looked over to the swaying, singing flesh on the floor and saw the man I had tricked with the night before. I couldn't even remember his name.

I took my present from Franny and left the Boatslip and went back to my room. I sat on the edge of my bed and opened the pad and drew a portrait of Franny. It was good.

FRANNY:

It was beautiful!

I just looked at that picture and knew it was beautiful. But it was still going to be hard with that boy. I knew that too.

I looked up at him and said, "You gotta earn that tea dance. From now on, I want a picture every day before you go show your butt to those men. Every day, mind you!"

JIMMY:

It was like learning to walk all over again. I don't know why I let Franny have that power over me. But it was as though he was a policeman. He wouldn't let me pass the intersection to the tea dance without my toll.

It was such a funny, strange kind of discipline. But it worked. I drew and drew and it got better and better. I began to tell people about my stuff and they'd come up to my room and look at it. It was as though my whole personality transformed itself. Franny was making me take myself seriously as an artist and so I was. And, as soon as I did that – took myself seriously – the rest of the people around me did too.

At the end of the summer I had a whole new portfolio. I didn't go to Key West that year; I stayed in Provincetown and worked at my drawing and began to paint again as well.

The next year I started to overhear people talking about me. I wasn't Jimmy-the-waiter anymore. I was Jimmy-the-artist. The whole world was different.

Franny & Stevie (1983)

STEVIE:

It was strange when I first saw Franny. Weird. I was looking at myself in the future. That was who I was destined to be.

I was a queen. No doubt about it. Everyone knew that since the day I popped out of my mother's belly. I looked like a queen. I acted like a queen. I felt like a queen. And I had hated every single, goddamned minute of it.

I had spent my whole life being hated and disdained. I looked at my parents and I saw their disappointment every time. I tried to make friends – and sometimes I could. But then I'd watch them become uncomfortable and worried and scared about what would other people think if they saw us together.

My life was to be alone. My only hope was to build up such a barrier that I couldn't be wounded. That became my life's ambition. I moved around the country trying to find the situation where there would be the least pain. It was all I could imagine happening.

I even thought about having my thing cut off. I went to a clinic in Minneapolis where they do the operation and told them I wanted to become a woman. That would make the rest of me make sense. But as I went through the counseling they make you do, I realized it couldn't happen. I was a queen, but I wasn't a woman.

I went to hairdressing school. What else? I could at least earn a living. I learned to put on makeup and cover the pit marks that made my skin as ugly as the world around me.

Then I went to Provincetown. It was a relief. There was a huge rock that was lifted up off my shoulders. The rest of the world is what seems strange when you live there. Not you. Them. They're the crazy ones. And I began to relax. If only a little bit.

ISADORA:

Everyone'd listen to Franny's stories. Everyone in the town. No question Franny had 'em all in the palm of her hand. The leather boys an' the muscle boys an' manly Joshua. But when that Stevie came to town it was somethin' else. Somethin' else again.

It scared me a little. Can't say it didn't. It was like Jay all over. This little queen Stevie who was so filled with the hate. The hate that kills. An' Franny was fallin' again. Fallin' just as hard. Sittin' on her porch and doin' more 'n tellin' stories. Feelin' more 'n just friendly an' concerned like with the others. Franny fell in love.

I was scared Franny was goin' to be crushed again. Just plain scared.

FRANNY:

No, no!

Stevie was different. I knew that right away. Stevie had only the fight in her. I saw that the first time that little thing walked down Commercial Street. She was wearing clothes that told the world just what she was and what she wanted them to see. Bright colors and fine lines and things that fit real good.

Oh, Stevie was different. Stevie was going to take what she had and she was going to *create* a place, one she wanted, not one someone else wanted for her.

JOSHUA:

It didn't take more than a couple days before Stevie was as much a fixture on Franny's porch as Franny himself. In a couple more weeks Stevie'd moved in. It took a while for everyone to adjust. Ted and

Fred and Terry had to get over some things. They were actually more than a little jealous if you asked me.

More than jealous though. They were used to this warmhearted "old man" who would give them a glass of lemonade and listen to their troubles and tell them stories and always be ready and willing to be supportive. Now there was someone else that was even closer to Franny than the rest of us were. That someone was frightened and cold and needed all the reassurance in the world that we weren't like every other person he had met. That he could relax and enjoy us and that we'd accept him as much as Franny did.

It just took time.

STEVIE:

I never doubted Franny. Not one minute did I doubt Franny. We understood the world together, as least the most important parts we saw the same way. But those men that would come around … I didn't know about the leather jackets that look like bikers and the muscles that looked like the jocks in school that used to tease me and beat me up. I had never been good for anything but a blow job to those other guys. How did I know these were any different?

If I was going to trust them, if I was ever going to know that they were on my side, there was going to be a good reason for it. I told Franny I didn't know about those other people. Franny I trusted. But them…?

JOSHUA:

Stevie would make some extra money cutting hair on the porch. Nothing big, certainly nothing big enough to make the real hair-dressers in town upset. But the guys who like Franny would come over and pay a couple bucks under the table and Stevie would cut their hair.

Franny would sit on a rocker beside them and tell Stevie each man's history. How Fred got muscles and how Ted used to dance and all the rest. That helped a little bit. For Stevie to hear that they had gone through something.

STEVIE:

Then one day I was walking back to the house with Fred and Terry. We had got something from the store. There was a pair of tourists standing on the sidewalk staring at Franny and laughing. Laughing! They made some comment about Franny being a queen.

I just blew.

"What the hell do you mean, 'queen'? That's no queen," I said, "that's the Queen of Provincetown!"

I said it so loud that Franny heard me and looked up. Isadora was walking to the house and she heard me too. Isadora yelled right back at me. "That's right, child, that's the Queen of Provincetown and I'm here to tell you that she done earned that title. She worked for that name and you don't let them forget it."

Terry and Fred just joined in and laughed the tourists right off the street, made them blush and nearly run away from us. I understood then I would've yelled anyway. And my words had power of their own. But with Fred and Terry and Isadora with me there was even more.

It was emotional for me. I was excited and frightened at the same time. I walked up the porch with my paper bag from the grocery and I looked at Franny. There were tears running down her cheeks. But not bad tears.

Franny looked up at me and stuck her chin in the air and said to me, "Don't you ever look back. Don't you ever."

Epilogue

Franny is the history of the development of the gay community.

It began with individual statements – Franny's sweater. It moved on to the strong friendships – Franny and Isadora. It then moved through tragedy – Jay's suicide. But something important had happened here. Franny, a *great* queen, had tried to intercede.

A climax in the book comes when Franny, Joel and Michael confront the internal homophobia of the gay community with the hiring of Jim.

Many people are surprised that the central character of the novel is a drag queen. They shouldn't be. Drags are usually portrayed as tragic figures in the gay world, but they were often its heroes. And its pioneers. They are the ones who settled our first ghettos and were often the ones who brought people together.

Franny in Provincetown is the composite of every wise queen I met there – and I went to Provincetown at least once every year of my adult life.

The book was published to some gratifying attention. However, I discovered a flaw in the first edition of the novel, which was that some of the language was inaccessible to many people. That only became apparent when I would read the book to audiences. This revision changes nothing from the original but makes the book more accessible by removing some of the harsher language.

Franny was one of the first gay male novels to present itself as such. Many people have asked what might have happened if *Franny* continued into the time of AIDS, but *Franny* was written and completed before the AIDS epidemic.

I imagine the scenario: many of the boys were trapped in the epidemic. Joshua left Franny his guesthouse. Franny, Isadora and Stevie turned it into a hospice. But that, too, is only something to be expected of a wise, compassionate queen.

– John Preston
Portland, Maine, 1994

Franny, Isadora, & The Angels

(A Working Draft)

A Note on the Text

It had been John's intention to write a second part to *Franny*, dealing with the AIDS epidemic, and his fervent wish to see it published together with a slightly revised version of the original text in a single volume, preferably in cloth. (The revisions to the original *Franny* were quite minor – mainly cleaning up some raucous street language that he had discovered, in his many public readings of the text, got in the way of people hearing the story.) He had been working on the new part for several months, in between bouts of his own illness, and had thirty-seven pages of manuscript – scenes and character sketches – but fretted that he had yet to find a story line to give the material shape.

In the last week of his life, after he got out of the hospital for the last time, he had enough energy to make the publishing arrangements for this new edition and sign a new contract, but unfortunately he did not have enough energy, or time, to complete the new text before he died in the early morning hours of April 28, 1994.

As his first and his last book editors, we have decided to include the new material in an appendix, under the title John had written on the manila folder containing the manuscript: "Franny, Isadora, & the Angles: A Working Draft."

These pages were still independent fragments and in no particular order, so we have arranged them in what appeared to us to be a sensible way and presented them basically as John left them, with very little editing. That *Franny*, John's first published book, should not only be the last work he prepared, but should remain unfinished due to AIDS is a sad testament to the dark times we are going through, and can stand as a permanent reminder of this remarkable generation of gay writers cut off in their prime by AIDS.

– *Michael Denneny and Michael Lowenthal*
October 6, 1994

Franny (1993)

FRANNY:

When he was alive, the Professor – he was my old man – used to tell me all about the way they thought up in that college where he taught, the one near Amherst. He explained to me that there were all kinds of fancy words you used, and then you'd be taken serious, if you knew how to talk. Me, I always needed to make noise to get heard. The Professor would do it different, he'd use their language.

But he also said there was certain ways of thinking, ways that have a lot to do with how you see things. You can just look and see nothing or else you can see the movement of history in the most simple thing. If you looked at it good and clear, and if you used the right words, well, you could explain all kinds of things to people. Like, the Professor used to say there was a natural history to sheets here in Provincetown. You just had to look closely and then you had to see how things worked.

First, the sheets were bought new by the New Yorkers, the people who owned the glitzy guesthouses right out on Commercial Street. They were worried that people might not think highly of them if it was discovered that they had old sheets, so they'd sell them off at the end of the season. The Yankees would buy them then and use them in their guesthouses, the ones that are more quiet and supposed to be more dignified. The thing is, the Yankees were cheap. They wouldn't be willing to just get a bargain on some perfectly good sheets. They'd want to make some money off them too. So, since they'd touched WASPY behinds, the Yankees would say that they weren't used sheets anymore, they were *heirlooms*. The tourists would buy them then for more than they cost new and take them home. It's an old Yankee trick. They take used furniture and they say it's antique so it's worth more. No, it isn't. It's the same old shit, it's still used furniture. But the Yankees said it was something special so the tourists would fall for it and pay good money for it. Hell, it's still used furniture to me. But everyone seemed to be happy about it.

But you see, that's how you got to look at the world. You and me, we might just wait till we go to J.C. Penny to buy us some sheets, and that says something too. It means that we have some sense in our minds, for one thing. Sense enough to laugh at the idea of how much the New Yorkers spend on sheets, just because some man with a Polo shop and a lot of plastic surgery says they're supposed to. And at the idea of the Yankees pushing those sheets off as heirlooms, just 'cause they farted on them.

But it tells you so much about people, to see how they treat sheets. The New Yorkers want to be able to answer the question if someone asks where the sheets come from. They want to be able to name the store and the designer. The Yankees, they're going to say, "They're heirlooms." The rest of us people don't expect to be asked.

I used to love to hear the way the Professor could take something like the way we use sheets and make it seem like the most important thing in the world, like it explained everything. He could write an article or something like that, I swear it's true, and get it published in one of those highbrow magazines of his.

At least that was the way it was when there was anything natural about history here. Everything's changed. Everything. There's a new chapter to the story. I treat sheets differently now, in a way that no one here ever expected. I stand outside the back doors of the most run-down guesthouses and I beg for their old sheets, even the ones the cheapest guesthouse owner would throw away because there are rips or holes in them.

You see, by the time a boy comes to my house, he's probably going to mess up a mountain of sheets. He's going to shit in his bed. Probably he'll bleed. Lots of times they throw up all over the place. I have to have an endless supply of sheets. The boys never care if they came from Bloomingdale's or Sears, Jordan's or Penney's, if they're old or new, torn or whole. When I get a boy, he only cares that they're clean.

And let me tell you something. *Listen to me!* Pay attention. When a boy comes to my house, *by God*, he gets as many clean sheets as he wants, as many clean sheets as he needs. Ten a day. Twenty. I don't care. I'll go beg for more if I have to. I'll wash them by hand if need be.

You know what? I'll even steal them. I will climb through the windows of every guesthouse in Provincetown and I'll clear out every linen closet in the place if that's what I need to do. When a boy comes to my house, I make him a promise. I promise him he will die in a clean bed.

Try and stop me from keeping that promise. Try it. Tell me no. Say you don't care. Tell me I'm too loud. Tell me I should go write a nice article like the Professor would. Tell me not to make noise. Try. *I dare you*.

It's 1993. And that's the natural history of sheets in Provincetown today.

❧

ISADORA:

From the beginning, Franny and I would haunt the corridors of the hospitals. We would roam up and down the hallways and we would listen for that sound, that sound that told us that some boy needed us. Or maybe it was a sight. Maybe it was the way someone looked. It could be the way the nurses talked about someone. We found the ones who needed us. We brought them back to this house.

FRANNY:

I did not do it because it was a charity! There is nothing charitable about watching someone die.

ISADORA:

Take it on home, maestro….

FRANNY:

It is an honor. It is the greatest honor that you can have, to be with someone who is dying. It the greatest gift that someone can give you, to allow you to sit in that room with them.

ISADORA:

Walk us out of here, moma….

FRANNY:

To think that there could be generosity involved in such an act that belongs to you, and not to that boy or girl! Why, they have *allowed* you to be there, at their most intimate moment, at the only thing more important than birth.

ISADORA:

Give me some traveling music, Franny….

FRANNY:

I am *honored* when they accept my invitation. I am *honored!*

ISADORA:

I'm not sure if I believe in God. But I do believe that other people believe.

I learned that everyone is capable of that belief one cold spring day when I was walking in Copley Square in Boston. I went into this gray stone Episcopal church there and there were all these other people. I never thought I would have anything to do with no Episcopals, they're so … white. But I was cold. So I sat down.

This woman stood up and the organ began to play and suddenly there was God coming out of her mouth, from deep down inside her.

I know that my Redeemer liveth …

She began that singing and I felt something come over me. Someone had written some music and that sucker had believed in God. I knew it when I heard that music. The white people in the choir knew it too.

I know that my Redeemer liveth …

Oh, my, what a surge I felt. Someone had seen something. Someone had felt something.

I sat there and listened to the white music and I felt God. Who ever thought that would happen to me?

Then – it seemed like minutes later, but it was a lot longer than that – they got to that place in the music where the whole lot of them stood up and began to sing.

Hallelujah! Hallelujah! Hallelujah! Hallelujah!
Lord God Omnipotent!

Where did that come from! I didn't know. But someone had believed in God.

The sound comes from all over the place. The Africans have this mass they wrote for themselves – none of that white shit. It's called the *Missa Luba*. I have records of it by these Kenya people and there's one by people from the Congo. We're talking darkest Africa. We are talking about people who don't know from cathedrals in Europe. But, child, listen to that music and you know that someone believed in God. Listen to the Sanctus in the *Missa Luba* and you know that there was no one faking it. Someone believed it was true.

FRANNY:
I knew all about God when I was growing up. I was born Irish Catholic. I had no choice. The man was always in my face. The thing is, when I came out and became a queen I learned I could talk back. That makes a difference, I tell you. That makes a big difference.

ISADORA:
Yeah, and once you found that out, you never have stopped yelling at him.

FRANNY:
And I ain't ever going to.

ISADORA:
I am a singer. In all the years I have been on the stage – and there have been many – I have never once lip-synched. I have always sung my music myself.

I can still sing it. I can sing the songs of the piano bar and make you remember your lost loves. I can sing disco and you'll think that you're back in the Saint at the Fillmore East. You'll smell the poppers, I can make it so real. Or give me a little house music and, honey, I will transport you to South Beach, Miami. Give me that *thumpa-thumpa* beat with all the soul of the Caribbean and I will make you see the gym-pumped bodies of the Warsaw Ballroom so clearly you'll want to lap the sweat off them. I swear, I can make you know those things with my music.

I learned to sing on my moma's lap, so you know I can sing gospel. You know that's the truth. The first song I ever heard my moma sing, least the first one I remember, was "Amazing Grace." Now that is a song that a singer can work! Moma used to scare me with those lyrics. There's one verse that holds all the truth about gospel in it:

> 'Twas grace that taught my heart to fear,
> And grace my fears relieved,
> How precious did that grace appear
> The hour I first believed.

Moma sang that and I shivered. I swear I did. Because she made me think that grace was something I couldn't have unless I believed the way her music did. I tried and tried when I was a little boy, just to believe for the sake of that music.

When Moma found out I was a queen, she took me in her arms and she sang another version, just for me:

> The Lord has promised good for me,
> His word my hope secures,
> He will my shield and portion be
> As long as life endures.

She sang that to tell me that grace was never to be taken from me. It was mine as a gift, that's the whole point of grace. You don't earn it by doing anything and you don't lose it just 'cause you're a queen. Grace *is*.

When all this started, I fell back to the basics. I will never forget the first time there was a boy here in the house that had that virus that makes them sightless. There seemed nothing else to do but sing this song to him.

Amazing grace! How sweet the sound
That saved a wretch like me!
I once was lost but now am found.
Was blind but now I see.

Oh, that child cried when he heard that song. He cried because he understood. Yes, he was blind, he was blind for the rest of his short life, but the song helped him understand that there was still something out there for him. He was *found* here at Franny's. He could never again see the sun off the harbor, but he could see the love.

When it's time, I sing the song for the children. I sing them over. I whisper in their ears at the end. It's a private thing, between me and them.

Through many dangers, toils and snares
I have already come;
'Tis grace hath brought me safe thus far,
And grace will lead me home.

Yes, yes, *lead me home!*
When it's over and I'm left alone, I still have a verse left for me:

When we've been here ten thousand years,
Bright shining as the sun,
We've no less days to sing God's praise
Then when we'd first begun.

Oh, Moma, if you only knew!

෨

MIKE:

But I'm only twenty-four! What the fuck do you expect me to do? I don't have the disease. I'm not going to get it. Who am I to say anything about it?

FRANNY:

I want you to take notes. Keep a journal. Paint pictures. Tell the stories. Sew a quilt. Wear a red ribbon. Talk about it!

ISADORA:

Play horns! Make noise! Break the silence!

FRANNY:

Join an organization! Feed the victims! Clean their houses!

ISADORA:

Comfort the afflicted!

FRANNY:

I want you to watch, to look, to remember. Sing songs about it. Make movies. Create videos. Petition the governor. Write letters to the editor. Picket the drug companies. March on the capitol.

ISADORA:

Testify!

MIKE:

It won't make any difference. I can't cure it. I can't stop it.

FRANNY:

But you must do all those things. You must observe it. Feel it.

ISADORA:
Act up!

MIKE:
But *why?*

FRANNY:
Because they are going to lie about it. They are going to tell lies about it. They are going to say it didn't happen. Or that it was the boys' fault. They are going to want to look away. They are going to want to think that it wasn't important. They will not admit their guilt. They will say it was an accident.

They are going to lie about it!

If you let them, they will never look in the mirror and see their own reflections. It will be what has happened to someone else. They won't see themselves.

MIKE:
It won't make any difference if I do a thing. They aren't going to believe me.

FRANNY:
Not unless you speak. Not unless you act. Not unless you demand they pay attention.

MIKE:
It's not my issue. I'm young. I'm healthy.

FRANNY:
You are harmed. Your life is made less whole. There is love that you will not experience, bodies you will not touch, hope you will not know. There are lessons you won't learn because the teachers are gone. There is wisdom that you will not receive. They have done this

to *you*, not to someone else, but to *you*. You don't have the disease you say? But there are people who think you are infected. There are people who are willing to diminish your life because of it. We all have a disease because of this plague, a disease of irresponsibility, a pestilence of avoidance.

You must not let this happen quietly. You must not allow it to happen softly. You must do something, something, *anything*. To be silent is to be dead. I know that. It's the knowledge of every queen in America. We know that.

ISADORA:
Can I find a witness?

The Flowers

ISADORA:

There was a hurricane that came through Provincetown during an autumn not too long ago. It was a mighty proof of the power of nature. The winds were so strong they moved the sand dunes right out over the highway. The waves washed away whole beaches. The rain flooded everything. This was a *storm*. It changed the very landscape. There were shutters flying through the air. Shingles ripped off roofs. Windows smashed open. I sat in the house and I quaked with fear. I was no match for a storm such as that.

When it was over I walked through Provincetown and looked at the devastation.

Everybody in Provincetown was heartbroken. The place looked terrible. Putting things back together was going to cost millions, and millions were already lost from the tourists who'd been warned away by the weather reports. Things were as dark as they ever got out here on the tip of Cape Cod.

But in a few days something began to happen. I was walking the streets of the village and I knew something had changed. I finally figured it out. The storm had come late in the fall, when the plants were going to sleep for the winter. But the winds had been from the South Atlantic, from wherever hurricanes are spawned. The rain had been tropical, warm and soaking. The hurricane had driven up water from the south. It had all fooled nature. What I had seen, what had been different, was that the plants thought it was a new spring. That powerful storm made them think it was time to grow again.

It began with the impatiens. They bloomed a second time that year. People didn't even have time to clear up their lawns and gardens, and there were the impatiens, sending up new flowers in the midst of the rubble. The rest of the plants followed.

We had seen the havoc wrought by that storm. The plants only knew it was warm and time to flower.

We gotta be like that. We have to live through the storm and look for the flowers. We have to be open to the miracle.

FRANNY:
Don't be giving me that nonsense. Don't you talk about the beauty of the plague. There is no beauty in this kind of death. There is no solace in this kind of loss. There is not one thing that has come out of this storm that could justify the loss of one young boy or girl. Not one thing.

ISADORA:
But maybe there will be more flowers, Franny. Maybe there will be new growth. We have to look for it.

FRANNY:
No! There are no miracles worth considering, not until there's a cure.

ISADORA:
There ain't never been a cure for a virus, Franny, not in the whole history of the world.

FRANNY:
Then think of the cure as the flower you're waiting to see in bloom. That's the only thing worth hoping for. I don't want any petals; I want medicine. I don't want nice words; I want action.

ISADORA:

We all be open to our miracles. It's the only way to let hope live.

Alan

ALAN:

I came to Provincetown for a vacation, Goddamn it! I asked my _friends_ where I should stay. There was only one place, they told me. You have to stay at Franny's.

I assumed I was going to be put up in a luxurious guesthouse. When I called and made the reservation and heard the price, I figured it damn well better be. This place wasn't cheap.

I flew out to Provincetown and took a cab from the airport. I got to the address and thought the place wasn't very impressive. It was just another of those Cape Cod houses. There wasn't even a swimming pool.

But it was too late at night to argue. I went in with my bags. When I first saw Franny I thought to myself, "This is a hairdresser gone bad." He wasn't really balding, but his hair was very thin. It was held in bondage by what must have been whole cans of hairspray. It wasn't quite a woman's bouffant, but you never saw hair like that in a men's locker room, I can promise you.

Where there should have been eyebrows, there were just thin penciled-on lines across his forehead. He had prominent pouch-like cheeks that were made all the more noticeable because he had rubbed a circle of cheap, rose-colored rouge on each one.

All right, so it wasn't going to be a fashion experience. I just told him my name and asked for my key.

"The rate's gone up to three hundred dollars a day," he said after I'd signed the registration card.

"What the hell do you mean? It was already highway robbery when you were charging me two hundred dollars."

He didn't miss a beat. "There's been a new boy moved in since then. Expenses have gone up."

"What kind of new boy is this, some kind of hustler I have to pay for?"

"No" – Franny busied himself with some paperwork – "he's from Taunton. Got that pneumonia three times in the past year. Doesn't look like he could survive another bout. He's going to be expensive."

"Why the hell should I pay for it?" I asked.

Franny looked up blankly and answered, "If you don't, who will?"

"This is not what I bargained for," I objected. "I wanted to come here for a vacation, not for – "

"You want a Holiday Inn, there's one out on Route Six." The voice was scathing. "You want a Provincetown event, you stay here, and it'll cost you three hundred dollars."

I don't know why I stood for it. I supposed I was tired from the trip. But I came up with the money and just asked him to show me where I was going to stay.

He led me up these rickety stairs to the third floor and opened a room for me. It was barren. I am not exaggerating. It had white walls and a bare wood floor. There wasn't even a bureau. Franny said, "There's shelves in the closet."

What was more eerie about it was that the only furniture was a plain single bed with white metal headboard and footboard. The only decoration came from empty picture frames on the white walls.

"You have to be the one that makes it pretty yourself," Franny said offhandedly. He went to the closet and bought out a big over-sized set of watercolors, the kind you can buy at Kmart. "You can paint the walls any way you want to. They're done with latex, so don't worry – I can clean it off later. Make your mark while you're here.

"I had one man who painted clouds all over the walls of this room. Big billowing clouds that looked wonderful when he was done. You would have thought this room was a piece of heaven then, he did it so beautiful. Another man found his demons. This room was covered with ugly faces and dripping blood. But it was his truth. You can do that too. Like I say, the walls are painted with latex and it will all wash off so the next person can make his own statement."

"I was told this place was a palace!" I snapped at him. "What kind of rip-off is this?"

"There's no rip-off," Franny answered. "This is my house. I am a queen. So this is a palace. What's your problem?"

Then he turned and left me in that room, left me to stare at the blank white walls and wonder just what I was supposed to do with them. Create heaven? Conjure up my demons?

The next morning I woke up and dressed and went downstairs. I had smelt the coffee being brewed in the common room and it lured me back to consciousness. I walked in and could see the pot on a warmer, but I couldn't just walk through.

The room was full of people. One man who was sitting in a wheelchair had an IV in his arm. Another seemed to be comatose, sitting in a hospital bed that had evidently been wheeled into the room. He was so gaunt I worried that he was already dead. There was a woman who had KS so badly her eyes were forced shut; she couldn't see. They sat there and all around them there were others who seemed to be just regular tourists, men in tight shorts and tighter T-shirts. No one seemed to pay attention to the hospital atmosphere or the sick people.

Then I realized that some of the others were sick themselves. There was one guy who didn't look bad at all until I saw the catheter built into his chest when he leaned forward to get some sugar and his shirt pulled back from the stretch. Another man looked absolutely healthy until you saw the telltale lesions on his thighs. I would have thought he'd cover them up, but he was wearing a Speedo bathing suit that exposed them, almost as though he were proud of them.

"You got a partial refund coming," Franny said when he finally brought me over a cup of coffee. I sipped it and marveled at how good it was.

"What do you mean, a *partial* refund?" I asked.

"That boy I told you about, he passed over last night. I won't be needing the extra money after all."

Franny reached into the pocket of this dreadfully bright caftan he was wearing and brought out two fifty-dollar bills and handed them to me.

If I had thought the things I'd seen were terrible, they were nothing compared to the idea that he was going to give me that money because a young man had died of AIDS. "Keep it," I said.

Franny didn't say a word. It was obvious he wasn't going to acknowledge this act of altruism on my part.

"I'm going to go to the beach," I said.

"Well … not quite yet, you're not." I looked over at the person who had spoken. It took me more than a moment to realize that it was a he. He was so beautiful and his makeup was so perfect that he must have been able to pass as a woman years ago. Now he was no spring chicken, but there was still an air of elegance and regalness about him.

He was black, with dark skin that seemed to be as smooth as the finest stone. He spoke with a deep, melodious voice. It was impossible to tell just how old he was. His skin was so perfect it denied aging. But there were streaks of white in his hair and deep crow's-feet around his eyes.

"That's Isadora. Helps me around here," Franny said.

"Been *helping around here* since that queen came out," Isadora scoffed.

"Well, I'm leaving," I said.

"Um, you better check with Franny before you go," Isadora said.

Franny picked up a clipboard and began to riffle through the papers. "Joshua over on Conant Street needs his dog walked. Then there's Micky over on Atlantic, he's got to have some prescriptions filled." Franny stopped reading and looked up at me. "You know how to start an IV?"

"No!"

"Surprising, during these times and all. We'll be able to show you how. Ever clean a Hickman catheter?"

"*No!*"

"Hmm," Franny said, passing judgment on my inadequacies. "Well, there's time for everything. Right now you just run those errands – I'll come up with a couple more things. You'll probably get to the beach in a couple hours. That's when the sun's best anyway."

All I wanted to do was get out of there. I thought I'd find another guesthouse, there had to be some cancellations someplace. I even thought about the goddamn Holiday Inn. *Anyplace.* But I couldn't move.

"It's the angels, isn't it?" Isadora suddenly said to me.

"I don't know what you mean," I said.

"Oh, yes you do. I can tell when it happens. You felt the angels last night, didn't you? You must have slept the sleep of the righteous. That happens when you feel the angels."

Isadora was right. I had had the most restful sleep of my life. I had climbed into the hospital bed and I had been furious – with Franny, with my friends for ever recommending this place, with all of it. But I had slipped quickly into sleep.

I dreamt about the clouds that Franny said the other guy had painted on the walls of the room. I floated in them. I heard music that could only have come from … angels.

"Angels happen when the spirits are at peace, after they cross over," Isadora said, rocking back and forth in his chair. "When the spirits can pass across in serenity, they like to linger. We give them all such love here, they like to stay after they're gone. They make the place calm."

I stood there and felt something move in my heart. I hadn't thought of my soul for years, but I knew it had been touched.

"Hell with you and your supernatural hogwash," Franny said angrily. "There are people who need to be taken care of on this earth and it's not going to happen if you all sit here and wonder about angels."

"I'm an angel," the woman with the bruised eyes said suddenly. She smiled in a peculiar way that made me think she suffered from dementia.

Franny's hard-assed routine was undermined. He stiffened a bit, then leaned over and kissed the woman's forehead. "Well, yes, dear. You *are* an angel."

Somehow I knew then that I would stay at Franny's. I took up the sheet of paper on which he'd written out the chores that had to be done and I left the house.

As I walked the streets of Provincetown that morning, my first thought was that I'd never slept with angels before and that I must be going insane if I thought I was doing it now. But then I remembered all the men who were gone – Pete, Charlie, Sam – all the men who I had slept with. For the first time I saw them, not as victims, but as angels I had known.

I was relieved and I was baffled. I didn't know what was really happening to me. I just knew I had to let it happen.

Alan

ALAN:

Isadora always told me that I should be thankful that I never saw Franny drive a real car. Franny evidently thought stop signs were for the unimaginative and speed limits were the burden of the overly restrained. Those were the nicest things Isadora had to say. Of course, I did see Franny drive his "cart."

He had this electric golf cart that he would use to go to the supermarket or run other errands in the village. The body was deep purple. It had a canopy that was lavender – I almost said "of course" right there. Needless to say, the reflector sign he had on the back of the cart to warn oncoming motorists was a huge pink triangle – and this time I will say "of course."

In case anyone didn't get the picture, Franny had two rainbow flags flying from the top of the cart, one on either side. This riot of color and political statement would maneuver its way through the crowded streets of Provincetown. It made a little *whir* sound as it moved, but if people didn't know Franny was coming there was a horn that sounded a strange *toot-toot*, like something you'd expect from a toy train, when he needed to warn you to make way for his royal procession.

The cart was pretty famous in Provincetown. Even if there were many eccentric people here, none of them approached Franny's flamboyance, and certainly no one could match the golf cart.

The sun in Provincetown is brilliant. The light comes down and bounces off the sand and off the water that surrounds almost all the town. Painters have told me that the light in Provincetown is perfect for their art. There is no place better in the world, they say, for making colors brilliant or shadows more intriguing.

The light wakes me up much earlier than I'm used to. I've learned to live with that. It's much better to get up at dawn here than to waste your time in dark, smoky bars. As soon as I started staying at Franny's I stopped fighting the light and climbed out of bed.

That's when I learned about Franny's special trips. I would look out my third-story window and I'd see Franny get into his cart and glide almost soundlessly through the deserted streets. I didn't really think much of it until I saw it many days in a row. I would smell the first whiffs of fresh coffee, then I would look out the window and see Franny driving away. He'd made the first pot, and then was gone.

I finally asked Isadora what it was all about. Where did Franny go at that hour?

Isadora tried to avoid the question, but I was insistent. I wanted to know.

"That's when Franny cries," Isadora finally told me. "He drives out to Herring Cove, before anyone else gets there, and he sits in the sand – whether it rains or no – and he cries. He cleanses his grief from himself for a while. Then he gets back in his cart and comes home.

"Franny promised that he would never cry in his own house while there were children dying here. Whatever grief he feels, he says it isn't worth their worry while they're sick. He goes off and does his own grieving, so when he comes back they don't have to worry about him."

I began to think of Franny's morning ritual as a kind of religious procession. I would stand watch and think of myself as the servant wishing the reverend well in his duties. Just as I had when I'd been an altar boy years and years ago. It was my own morning rite, to stand in the window and watch Franny go to cry.

Kris

FRANNY:

Well, I was driving my cart back from the store and Isadora was with me. Now that is a person who can backseat-drive. Every time you do the slightest thing wrong, well, she starts squawking and carrying on and you just want to slap her face.

So I was turning onto Commercial Street and there he was, sitting there on a lawn chair with his legs spread open and ... well, I just lost control of myself and the cart. I ran it right into a telephone pole. I could imagine what Isadora was going to say about *that*.

But she sat there calmly for a change, just looked at me, then at him, then back at me and said, "It was a God thing."

It was obvious that Isadora agreed this was the most beautiful boy in the world. 'Course, he would know it himself, too.

KRIS:

The best way to understand what I look like is to think of an updated version of Michelangelo's David. I am classical beauty, circa 1993. Here, let me take off my shirt and show you.

Notice the arms first. My biceps have a pleasant roundness to them, carefully maintained in the gym, of course. My triceps are a bit tighter – don't you think the cut look there is effective? But none of this is overdone. There isn't a hint of steroids here. This is natural beauty.

There are some things that you can't force. There are some things that you get from your gene pool and all you can do is thank your parents. Look at my nipples. They're not too large, but they're nicely perky, don't you think?

Of course the pectorals they sit on had to be developed carefully, to give my nipples the most perfect frame. Then my torso sweeps down onto what you have to admit is a nicely flat stomach. It's hard to keep in such good shape that your abs are always defined – and mine are.

I'm not into exhibitionism of the sexual sort, at least not in public, at least not at the moment, so the pants stay on. Suffice it to say that what's underneath them complements the rest quite nicely. As do my legs. It took a lot of time and effort to get the thighs to look just so. The calves were torture. Any bodybuilder can tell you that the worst thing of all is working on your calves. It may be that it has to do with genes, that you can only have well-developed calves if you have the right genes. As you can see, I have more to thank my parents for.

This body is too important to me to let hair stand between it and you. I shave the whole thing, except for a small, tasteful triangle over my crotch. I want you to see everything my family tree and my gym sweat have created. There are no tattoos, of course not, and no piercings. They would interfere with the aesthetic experience that is me.

I know I'm attractive, and I know that's obvious to everyone. I am the man the bouncer at the hottest club lets in the door without an invitation. Strangers have walked up to me on Commercial Street and asked to buy my underwear, just as a memento of the first time they saw me. A Hollywood producer skipped over the casting couch shtick and just handed me a blank check to spend the night with him.

But the attention comes only because they don't know that I'm infected. It sort of changes your concept of beauty when you find out that this body you lust for could kill you. And I could. I have virulent strains of exotic diseases coursing through my body. I am an invitation to a medical textbook's worth of illnesses. I am an open door to death.

But don't worry about that right now. Let me pose for you. Let me work up a little sweat, maybe you'd like to lick it off. Or does that frighten you, the thought of my bodily fluids? It makes you crazy, doesn't it, to want something as dangerous as me. It probably makes you craziest to know that you do still want me, even now that you know. I am a demon of death, a horseman of destruction, the vanguard of the cataclysm. I am your worst nightmare.

ISADORA:
Franny looked at the boy and she saw an angel. That's all there was. We knew from his sadness that he was sick, no matter how good he looked. Franny got up out of the cart and walked over to him and apologized for the accident, even though we'd been going so slow nothing had been hurt.

Franny ignored me and sat down next to Kris and started to talk to him, the way he does. He always goes back to the beginning, to the time when they were little boys. He wants to know about their childhood, 'cause he wants to know what they're really frightened of. You don't ever know that until you know what happened to someone when he was a baby.

Franny sat there and talked to this living statue and finally brought him home with us. They was bonded, that's the term people use nowadays. It was just like the old days when Franny would adopt boys, bring them into the house and save them. The only difference is, there's not much to do to save them these days. You can't do it. All you can do is make them into angels.

Alan

ALAN:

I had been on the coast, doing some legal work out there. When I flew back to Provincetown everyone told me – the clerk at the airport, the cab driver, they all knew.

I flew up the stairs to Franny's room. I had never been inside it. It was an inner sanctum to my mind, the one place where privacy ruled in that house.

I threw open the door and there was Mike, playing his horn. He never looked up at me, he just kept on playing some kind of funereal music that did seem to have a strange beat to it. I realized later that it was a dirge from New Orleans, something the jazz bands would play while the corpse was taken for burial.

Franny sat in a big overstuffed chair and seemed to stare out into space, just letting the music glide over him.

"Kris?" That was all I could say.

"It happens quick sometimes. The virus gets into their brains. He had seizures that were terrible, the worst I've ever seen. The first time was bad. He wasn't in good shape afterwards. Then they came back again. And again. We did everything we could, but there was no fighting anything like that."

"How are you, Franny?" I finally asked.

"I do not cry in this house," Franny said without looking at me. Of course, I knew that was against his own rules, but for once I wished he'd break them. I wished he'd let himself go.

Mike's music kept sweeping over us. I couldn't help noticing the room, this sanctuary of Franny's which I'd never seen anyone else enter before. It was stunning, but not in the way you might expect.

There was a fireplace in one wall. All around it were photographs, most of them very small, just wallet-sized. Some were in cheap frames that you might buy in a supermarket, ersatz pewter. Others were in what were rough, obviously handmade frames that made you think of summer camp and the fumbling hands of little boys learning how to build things for the first time. Some were only Scotch-taped to the surface; a few were held in place by pushpins.

"I have always thought that every person in the world should know that his picture is over someone's mantel," Franny said, seeing my interest. "I suppose it's because I was never sure I had one of my own anywhere for so long. When I came here to Provincetown I was determined that everyone would have a place over my mantel. It was the least thing I could do for them."

Kris was already there. "But there are such wonderful pictures of Kris," I complained. "I'll have one of them professionally matted for you. I'll get a perfect frame – "

"That one *is* perfect," Franny said sharply.

It was a snapshot of Kris wearing a small bathing suit. It had evidently been taken before he had begun his campaign to be flawless. There was a bit of hair on his chest, which wasn't as prominent as when I first met him. He seemed younger, less polished. His hair was a bit too full, too long. His smile was innocent, something I realized I had never seen on Kris in all the time I had known him – innocence. Franny was right, this was the perfect photograph.

I looked at the rest of them. I wondered at the spectrum of humanity. There were probably hundreds of gay men. They came in every color, were of every age, seemed to be of every background.

Franny got up from his chair and came over to point to one of them. He appeared to have a shaved head; his face seemed a mask of fear. "That was my first. That's Sydney. He lived down in New York.

He got it before they had a name for it, before there was any head-lines or anything like that.

"Sydney kept on getting sick. The doctors didn't know what the hell was happening to him. They said, 'What foreign country have you been to?' They asked that because he had these tropical diseases that you only got if you went to Asia or Africa, and then you had to go deep into the bush. Truth was, Sydney had never been west of New Jersey or east of Fire Island, so they couldn't figure it out at all.

"This was – oh, it might have been as early as 1977 that Sydney started to get sick. He was in and out of the hospital all the time. He kept having to go to this special clinic for infectious diseases they had up in the Bronx. He complained about that the most, having to go up to the Bronx to see a doctor that couldn't even give a name to what was ailing him.

"Sydney had always been a sort of bitter queen. The sicknesses didn't help that. But he had been a good person. He had been an artist of sorts. He worked with that Charles Ludlam, the one that did all the revolutionary shows – *Camille* and things like that in drag. Sydney helped out with the makeup and the dresses and all.

"He finally passed over. We were sad of course, but no one knew then what was going to happen. No one knew what the toll was going to be.

"The babies," Franny said pointing to small photographs of black infants, "they're Haitian. A priest came to us and said we had to help. Isadora and I went nuts. We went and got baby furniture from the Salvation Army and set up a nursery and the whole thing. We convinced a Portuguese fisherman to go down and pick them up in his boat.

"We smuggled them into the country. We carried those babies ashore in our own arms so the immigration wouldn't catch us. We started out down in Haiti with a dozen children. Just beautiful children. Didn't they have the blackest skin! By the time we got back here to Provincetown, there were only two left. Just two.

"Isadora loved those babies. We didn't have much of a chance to appreciate them, though. They died early.

"We'd take more of them. The bassinets and such are still in the basement if we need them.

"The women," he spread his hand over the left part of the wall, where I could see dozens of women's pictures, "are mainly working girls. Whenever we have room, Isadora and me get someone to drive us down to Fall River and New Bedford, to the really poor parts of town. There are always working girls there who know it's time to come and take a rest, who know they need us. We give them all the dignity they deserve.

"But it's the boys, of course," Franny seemed to take in all the photographs on the wall. "We started because of the boys."

I could imagine that there had once been only a few photographs over the mantel. I could see how they had cascaded down the sides of the fireplaces. Franny must have gotten a ladder to put up the ones at the top of the wall, by the ceiling. And it must have been a cruel moment when the space the photographs took began to crawl onto the other walls.

There was no end to the photographs, I understood then.

Mike's horn continues to play its soft and melodic tune.

"Everyone should know that there's a mantel with his photograph on it." That was all that Franny would say. I looked over to see if he would break his rule, but he didn't. Franny refused to shed a tear while he was still in his house. We stood there and listened to Mike's horn and looked at the pictures, all the pictures as they streamed over the mantel and over the walls.

Appendices

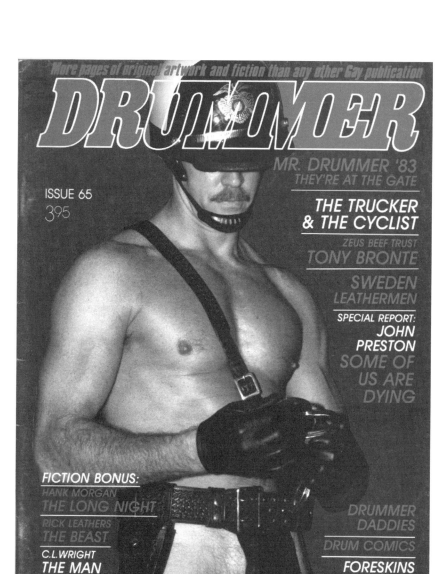

More pages of original artwork and fiction than any other Gay publication

DRUMMER

MR. DRUMMER '83
THEY'RE AT THE GATE

ISSUE 65
3⁹⁵

**THE TRUCKER
& THE CYCLIST**

ZEUS BEEF TRUST
TONY BRONTE

SWEDEN
LEATHERMEN

SPECIAL REPORT:
**JOHN
PRESTON**
SOME OF
US ARE
DYING

FICTION BONUS:
HANK MORGAN
THE LONG NIGHT
RICK LEATHERS
THE BEAST
C.L.WRIGHT
THE MAN
JARRED SCOTT
LUST

DRUMMER
DADDIES
DRUM COMICS
FORESKINS
DRUMBEATS
CLASSIFIEDS

From *Drummer* magazine, Volume Seven, Number 65 (June 1983)

Queens Rule

by John W. Rowberry

To more than a few people, John Preston's second book, *Franny The Queen of Provincetown* (Alyson Publications, trade paperback, 1983) is going to come as a complete and total surprise. I mean, after *Mr. Benson*, who would suspect that Mr. Preston had such a book in him – yearning to be free?

Franny is what could politely be called an old world queen, born of the stereotypical Eisenhower era, trapped in a netherworld of gender misidentification, seemingly destined to live life between bar raids and social scorn.

But make no mistake, Franny is not the story of a pathetic pre-liberation gay man trying to pass himself off as a demi-woman. Instead, Mr. Preston has found a convincing way to delineate much of what 'liberation' is all about. *Franny* is a strikingly original testimonial to greatness of character that might remind more than a few of us where we came from.

Franny travels not only through specific times and places (the beginnings of the modern gay liberation movement, the emerging 'resorts' of newly-liberated gay men) but through personas – a character evolving until, by the brief book's end, we are in the presence of what can only be described as a whole person, for better or for worse. It is the kind of theme that Andrew Holleran and Larry Kramer used as the foundation of their well-known books, but here it works: quickly, quietly, exceedingly well. John Preston has suddenly shown a leap of growth of a novelist.

From *Something Inside: Conversations with Gay Fiction Writers*
by Philip Gambone, University of Wisconsin Press, 1999
(The interview took place on September 25, 1993)

It was soon after your move to Portland that you wrote what you call your first novel, Franny, Queen of Provincetown, *a series of dramatic monologues by an aging avocado-shaped queen, who manages to be both tough and bighearted. Such a novel from the "dark lord of gay erotica" seems kind of anomalous. What was behind your decision to write* Franny?

I love the fact that you point out that Franny was an avocado-shaped queen. I really learned so much in writing *Franny*. I don't know if you're aware of this, but that is literally the only description of Franny in the book. I was amazed to watch reviewers talk about the "wonderfully realized character" who was an avocado-shaped queen. But there is not another word that physically describes Franny in the whole book. So that was an intriguing lesson about the effect of minimalism.

I did not perceive of myself as a writer – you must always remember that – when I wrote *Franny*. Or I was only beginning to perceive of myself as a writer, and the basic way I had that was this phenomenal audience response from *Mr. Benson* and the other sex writing I had done. And my immediate response to that response was, Oh, I can write anything for these kids, these guys. And it was the response of my editors that I could write anything. I never felt restricted to what I had been writing. I very quickly, for instance, moved to essays, and published essays in *Drummer*, which everyone had thought would be an impossibility.

As most often in my writing, *Franny* was motivated by anger. There was a spate of books then – this was about 1982 – where it became almost mandatory for the gay male author to kill the drag queen.

The drag queens were the great victims in many gay books. It's almost as though we were trying to kill off the repressed image of what it meant to be a gay man and create the clone. I've never seen that actually explored – and I don't intend to go back and reread all those terrible first novels – but it was certainly my response that these were heroes, not victims. I wanted to prove what heroes they were and to show how they were heroes. So I created Franny and Isadora, his sidekick, who essentially become the mentors of young gay men as they come out.

On this, the eve of the twenty-fifth anniversary of Stonewall, I think it will be emphasized again and again that it was, in fact, drag queens at the Stonewall Inn who started that riot on the night of Judy Garland's funeral.

Yeah, but it will probably be emphasized again and again in ballrooms and in the Grand Hyatt. You know, it's a lot easier to validate the idea of a drag queen as opposed to living with the drag queen.

Let's talk about the Alex Kane novels. There are six such novels, under the heading "The Mission of Alex Kane," which you wrote in the mid-eighties. First of all, who is Alex Kane?

Well, there's background that we should talk about. I wrote and published *Mr. Benson*, *Franny, the Queen of Provincetown*, and *I Once Had a Master* in a relatively short period of time. They all came out as books within the same twelve months. I'd written these books and had moved to Maine with the purpose of becoming a writer, exploring this new possibility. One of the first things that happened was I realized I was taught quite cruelly, that I was not going to earn a living as a writer of gay material. The money I received for those books was $500 for *Mr. Benson*, and $750 for *Franny*. This was not going to work. I also knew from the experience of one of my great role models, who was Samuel Steward, and also from my understanding of myself, that I was not going to be a writer unless I lived as a writer, that if I so much as attempted to have a part-time job it would just be in my personality that I could not focus on being a writer. So it was very important for me to live as a writer.

From *Lambda Book Report*, Volume 3, Issue 4 (May 1992)
Preston on Publishing: Building Libraries … with Help from Mom
[excerpt]
by John Preston

When I published my first novel, *Franny the Queen of Provincetown* (Alyson), I was already living in Portland, Maine. My mother came here to attend a regional meeting of New England town clerks. Without telling me what she was doing, she arranged for me to come to her hotel room for a drink. A single gin-and-tonic is usually her limit when it comes to alcohol, but there were many bottles of liquor on her bureau. And the room was much more elegant than I'd have expected her to rent; ostentation isn't one of her vices. I didn't understand what was happening until one by one the town clerks of New England – almost all of them ladies, almost all of them with Republican hair – marched into the room to meet Nancy's son-the-author over a friendly cocktail. That the book dealt with an aging dragqueen fighting for the dignity of gay men didn't matter. My mother's son had written a novel and, by God, she was going to celebrate.

Drag Queens, Leathermen, and Telling the Truth:
Franny and the Life of John Preston
by Dusk Peterson

In 1973, a reporter for *The American Baptist* interviewed a young, long-haired, Christian gay activist. The activist told the reporter, "You expect a perverted, evil effeminate person with unnatural lusts. But, believe me, most homosexuals are incredibly normal people."

Ten years later, John Preston's *Franny, the Queen of Provincetown* was published by Alyson Books. How, in the space of ten years, had Preston gone from associating effeminacy with evil to writing a sympathetic novel about a drag queen?

To start the story, we must go back to the early 1960s, when a teenager hung around Boston's Park Square, seeking men with whom to have sex. Years later, Preston was sure he knew the reason why he managed to escape the dangers faced by others who had taken the same route. "I was guarded by a flock of black drag queens who just loved to mother a young boy from the country," he said. "No one let me go with any of the men who might be dangerous. I was not allowed to go into places where there would be people using hard drugs. I had my swarm of queens around me to make sure I went only with the right men."

A more orthodox role in the gay community lay ahead of him. In 1969, having graduated the previous year from a college near Chicago, Preston moved to Minneapolis and became part of the thriving gay rights movement there. He came out of the closet as a gay man and threw himself into various projects, such as co-founding a gay community center and publishing a sexual health newsletter for gays. In 1974, he helped edit a newsletter for a New York City sexual education organization, SIECUS. And in 1975, he became editor of *The*

Advocate, a California gay newspaper (later newsmagazine), with the result that he was quoted in *Newsweek* magazine.

Yet Preston was still deeply in the closet. He presented himself to the press as an average citizen: a committed Episcopalian ("I'm on a heavy religion trip," he told activist Jack Baker around 1969), a student of theology and health, and a man who had applied successfully for federal funds for his work. He joined other mainstream gays in condemning anything that might threaten the gay rights movement, such as bisexuality or the use of gay pornography in educational materials. (Ironically, Preston would later help pioneer the use of pornography as a tool for safe sex education.)

His condemnation of effeminacy to the *American Baptist* reporter was part and parcel of this image-making. As far back as the 1950s, many gay activists had distanced themselves from queens in an effort to provide a model of homosexuality that the average American could accept. Preston, working to change attitudes toward homosexuality by his fellow Christians, did the same. He tried to convince the press that he was not in the least bit "unnatural."

He did not tell the press that he was a leatherman.

Preston later said that his first acquaintance with gay sadomasochism came during his college years, when he began visiting the Gold Coast in Chicago and other leather bars. Preston found that the masculine emphasis in leather touched him deep inside. "S/M sex was a way many of us explored the most profound elements of ourselves," he later wrote about those bars. "Men who had been told all their lives that they were frail queers suddenly found themselves in places where they could confront themselves as strong and resilient."

For Preston – both in his life and in his writings – the most powerful image the leather world had to offer was of an older man initiating a younger man into manhood through a trial of endurance. The older leatherman, Preston said, "is passing on the ancient rites of the tribe. He is making sure that the passage to malehood is done appropriately and with ample regard to the rules of the clan."

But the rites chosen by leathermen were in direct contradiction to the rites thought acceptable by mainstream society. In 1982, Preston told how an acquaintance was aghast after witnessing Preston "debase" another man in an SM session at the Mineshaft bar. Preston reported, "I could hardly find the words to explain it to someone who obviously hadn't understood what had gone on between the first man and myself. I had offered him a trial, an initiation, a chance to test himself against real forces of adversity. He had chosen to trust me to provide that. I had come through for him and he for me."

If Preston could be misunderstood by someone visiting a bar where sexual activity openly took place, the barriers to explaining himself to more conservative folks must have seemed insurmountable. In 1991, Preston spoke about the tension that lay between leathermen and early gay activists, a tension that may have been reflected in his own life. "The first impulse of gay activism, to be a form of progressive and even revolutionary politics, was left behind. In the place of that rebellious attitude, there was an almost immediate plea for social acceptance."

By contrast, he said, "The original leather bars were places where men could gather, and … say: *In your face!* Leather was gay sexuality stripped of its being nice. It offended. It confronted. It took sex as its own ultimate value. It was a reaffirmation of the revolution, not a dilution of it."

At the end of the 1970s, Preston made his choice between the world of mainstream gay activism and the world of radicals. In later years, he would often speak with amusement about how a staff member at the gay leather magazine *Drummer* persuaded him to use a pseudonym for what would become his most famous novel, *Mr. Benson*, an SM love story. But Preston failed to mention that, even before *Mr. Benson* was serialized in *Drummer*, he had begun to write pieces for that magazine under his real name. Around the beginning of 1979, Preston came out of the closet a second time when his name appeared in *Drummer*, attached to an erotic story about a boot store and leather art gallery in New York City.

Although Preston had abandoned mainstream gay activism, he had not abandoned mainstream Americans. In 1979, he moved to Portland, Maine, and took great pride in the fact that he was able to establish friendly relations with his more conservative neighbors. To the end of his life, Preston would continue to live in tension between his desire to embrace the good he saw in the world of radical sexuality and his desire to reach people in mainstream society. He was remarkably successful in both areas, writing books that won him awards from mainstream organizations at the same time he was continuing to turn out popular books of leather pornography. By the early nineties, he had merged both his worlds by editing a series of gay erotic fiction anthologies for a major press.

Yet in one respect, Preston had never faced a choice. Both the mainstream gay community and the leather world were agreed on a single issue: effeminate men should be turned away at the door.

In the case of the leather world, this "turning away at the door" was often literal. In the late seventies and early eighties, the most famous place to go in order to have leathersex was the Mineshaft, an afterhours bar in New York City. Preston was certainly familiar with the

Mineshaft. He wrote about it in *Mr. Benson* and in a 1993 essay entitled "The Theater of Sexual Initiation." Michael Shernoff, a New York gay activist in the seventies, remembers encountering Preston there one night, giving a tour of the place to a man whom Shernoff later learned was none other than the French philosopher Michel Foucault.

The Mineshaft's dress code was equally famous. "Approved are [motorcycle] & Western gear," it proclaimed. "No cologne or perfume or designer sweaters."

The Mineshaft was hardly alone in its disdain of "girlish" clothing. In 1964, *Life* magazine described the decor of a San Francisco leather bar, the Tool Box: "A cluster of tennis shoes – favorite footwear for many homosexuals with feminine traits – dangles from the ceiling. Behind it a derisive sign reads: 'Down with sneakers!'"

The leather world's dress codes had many purposes, among them to create an atmosphere of intense masculinity. A necessary side effect of this was that these dress codes barred effeminate men from entering leather establishments. Most leathermen were, if anything, even more hostile to queens than mainstream gays were, for gay leather had been founded in reaction to the widely held belief that all homosexuals must be queens.

In only one place could effeminacy be regularly found in the leather world: the drag shows held by leathermen's motorcycle clubs provided high camp that allowed club members a brief release from their usual hypermasculine imagery. As in other masculine societies such as the military, these drag shows were performed, not by queens, but by masculine men. "In fact," leather author Joseph W. Bean points out, "the men in the shows made a mockery of effeminacy and probably had more effect in underscoring the division [between queens and leathermen] than in bridging the gap."

We return to the question, then: Why was Preston's reaction to queens so different from that of many of his contemporaries? After spending so many years among gay activists who condemned effeminacy, and among leathermen who condemned effeminacy, why did Preston write a sympathetic novel about a drag queen?

At least part of the answer must lie in Preston's early contact with drag queens and his remarkable ability to connect their experiences with the experiences of leathermen.

"Once you have entered this arena," he said, speaking of a willingness to take on a gay sexual identity, "you embrace the identity of the outlaw so fervently, there is no reason to establish boundaries.... It's not too different from a process that many observe in many transvestites who are gay men. If you are going to go so far as to challenge the male stereotype by admitting and demonstrating your homosexuality, you might as well go all the way and reverse the expression of your gender. You have already attacked the assumptions of your gender so vigorously by being homosexual, there is no reason to stop with that. That's certainly the position of many transvestites who infuse their cross-dressing with political motivations...."

For the leatherman, Preston went on to suggest, the equivalent to this process is using sadomasochism as a way to establish one's masculinity. Both the leatherman and the drag queen are rebelling against society's proscribed boundaries for them; they have simply chosen different ways in which to do so.

The reception of *Franny* in the leather community was surprisingly friendly, perhaps because its reviewers in *Drummer* and the gay SM newsletter *DungeonMaster* were all friends of Preston. John W. Rowberry, assistant publisher of *Drummer* at that time, made sure his readers understood that *Franny* was not a capitulation on Preston's part to the idea that gay men *must* be effeminate. "Make no mistake," he said, "Franny is not the story of a pathetic pre-liberation gay man trying to pass himself off as a demi-woman. Instead, Mr. Preston has found a convincing way to delineate much of what 'liberation' is all about."

Similarly, leather author T.R. Witomski quoted Franny's speech to a leatherman: "Now don't go and get upset at an old queen like me when I say this, but what you got on is drag just as sure as my fanciest ball gown. But that's good. That's being creative and that's making your own way in the world and not letting someone else tell you how you should be...."

In an unexpected turn of events, Preston himself fell afoul of leather dress codes in later years, when he insisted on showing up at leather gatherings wearing sweaters. "Don't you know who this is?" exclaimed a companion of Preston's, witnessing him being turned away from attending a Mr. Leather contest. "This man wrote *Mr. Benson!*"

"Ah, the magic title!" Preston later commented in a dry manner. "Administrators were called over, and the door opened." For Preston, this was evidence of how many leathermen had begun to mistake the trappings of radical sexuality for the heart of it.

But his greatest scorn was reserved for folks who continued to believe that gay men would be accepted by society "if only you wore the right clothes." This belief Preston described as a "haunting" and "insufferably painful" memory of a "desperate hope" for acceptance that lay in the past.

His past, perhaps?

Toward the end of his life, Preston wrote a series of articles condemning people who wished to make all of gay life palatable to mainstream society. His words in "Gay Pride, Telling the Truth, and Pornography" not only criticize other gays whom he considered to be appeasers. His words also condemn the young gay activist who earnestly told a reporter that he was "incredibly normal."

> Whether it's in Boston, Minneapolis, Portland, or anywhere else, there is one perpetual problem [with gay pride celebrations]. A dark shadow always comes into the midst of this carnival, this innocent festival of carnal togetherness. It's nothing less than an attack on the people who come together to live it up, and it's not an attack by the religious right. It comes from the supposed leaders of the gay community who begin to bellyache about the "irresponsibility" of some of the participants, the way those participants "act out" stereotypes that make it seem that gay men are too sexual or that drag queens and leathermen are too prominent in "the community." These "leaders" get angry that these "negative forces" are giving the press fodder to make "the community" look bad. If we would only "behave," we would be able to get our civil rights, they insist. If we presented ourselves as being "stable" citizens, then their organizations would be able to maneuver better in the political world. If we wear leather or dresses or hardly anything at all, the "leaders" won't be able to control how "our cause" is handled.
>
> I want to scream. I want to yell. *What the fuck do these people think it's been all about! Why do they think those of*

us who started this whole thing took the risks we took, the chances we gambled? We didn't do it so a lot of white boys could make careers lobbying in Congress or could assuage their own insecurity by showing off a perfect community to their social-worker friends. We did it because....

We did it so that drag queens could march down Boylston Street and not get beaten up. We did it so leathermen and leatherwomen could spend an afternoon at the park and not feel like freaks. We did it so young boys and girls could come to a gathering of tens of thousands of people and could see someone who was hot enough that the very lust they felt was a reasonable justification for coming out.

We did it so we could be honest about ourselves and not feel ashamed. We did it because we knew that secrets are our most deadly enemies, and telling the truth is our strongest weapon.

Notes

I would like to express my thanks to Robert Guenther, who reminded me of the leather tradition of drag shows, and to Joseph W. Bean, who immediately responded to my plea for a quick critique of this essay. Neither man, of course, is responsible for any remaining errors in the essay.

Preston's remark about evil effeminates was printed in the June 1973 issue of *The American Baptist*. He discussed his experiences as a teenager in Boston in *My Life as a Pornographer* (see below) and in various passages in *Hustling* (Masquerade/Richard Kasak, 1994). His comment that he was on "a heavy religion trip" is quoted in Robert Halfhill's remembrance, "John Preston Joins an Organization of Gay Students," which, along with Michael Shernoff's remembrance about Preston at the Mineshaft, is available in *Topman's Timeline: A Documentary Biography of John Preston*, edited by Dusk Peterson (2004-present; online at *www.prestonproject.org*). Preston's remarks about bisexuality and gay pornography in educational materials appeared in "Unitarian Sex Courses Biased, Critic Charges," *The Advocate* 84 (April 1972), page 14. Preston's comments on the "degrading" SM session were published in his essay, "One Confession of What Turns a Top On," in *DungeonMaster* 20 (1982), page 11. The Mineshaft dress code is quoted in Leo Cardini's introduction to his *Mineshaft Nights* (FirstHand, 1990), while the Tool Box was described in Paul Welch's "Homosexuality in America," *Life* (June 26, 1964). The remarks by Joseph W. Bean on drag shows are quoted with his permission from private correspondence to this author, dated July 21, 2005. The reviews of *Franny* by Rowberry and Witomski are: John W. Rowberry, "DrumMedia Books," *Drummer* 65 (1983), page 72; T.R. Witomski, "DrumMedia Stage: *Franny* Opens in New York," *Drummer* 79 (1984), page 99.

All other quotations by Preston are from his essay collection, *My Life as a Pornographer and Other Indecent Acts* (Masquerade/Richard Kasak, 1993). The page numbers for those quotations are as follows: "I was guarded" (152), "S/M sex was a way" (128), "Passing on the ancient rites" (62), "The first impulse" (127-28), "Once you have entered" (59), "'Don't you know'" (126), "If only you wore" (178), and "Whether it's in Boston" (150-51). Preston's "The Theater of Sexual Initiation" also appears in that volume.

Excerpt from John Preston's C.V., 1993

Special note about *Franny, the Queen of Provincetown*:
Franny was written as a novel and presented to the book-buying public as such. But its structure of interlocking monologues lent itself easily to stage adaptation and, in fact, it not only was named The Gay Novel of the Year by The Front Page when it was published, the same year it won the Jane Chambers Memorial Award as one of the best gay plays of the year.

These are the productions of *Franny* to date:
Ogunquit, Maine – A staged reading from the author's adaptation, 1982.

New York City – A production based on an adaptation by Bert Michaels for the Meridien Theatre Company, 1985.

Boston – A production based on an adaptation by Robert Pitman for the Triangle Theatre Company, 1985.

Houston – A production based on an adaptation by Joe Watts for the Pink Triangle Theatre, 1986.

San Francisco – A staged reading held at the Walt Whitman Bookstore from an adaptation by Robert Pitman, 1986.

St. Louis – A production sponsored by the gay community based on an adaptation by Gil Seaman, 1988.

Phoenix – An independent production based on an adaptation by Steve Schemmel, 1988.

Rochester – An independent production, 1991.

Editor's Note: We had hoped to include an excerpt from the play adapted, as it was, from this novel and enlisted the help of many people connected with its various productions in our search. Our research led us to individuals and archives in Los Angeles, San Francisco, Chicago, New York, Boston, Provincetown, and Ogunquit. Lots of people knew all about the play's history, but no one seemed to have easy access to the text. No doubt, copies of the adaptations and even the stage scripts exist in filing boxes and storage units out there somewhere, and we hope these texts might appear in a future printing of this edition.

From *Drummer* magazine, Volume Nine, Number 79 (1984)
Franny in New York
by T.R. Witomski

The Meridian Gay Theatre opened their 1984–85 season with an adaptation of John Preston's *Franny, The Queen of Provincetown*. Preston, a writer near and dear to the hearts (and other places) of *Drummer* readers, shows another aspect of his talent in *Franny*. We always knew that that author of *Mr. Benson* could turn us on; with *Franny*, Preston shows he can make us laugh and cry too.

Franny, in a series of short scenes, spans some thirty-odd years in the life of "the ugliest bitch I ever did lay my eyes on … Franny would have looked like a queen if you dressed him in full leather." Attempting to be nothing less than a social history of American gays from 1950 to the present, *Franny*, as Preston noted in the novel's epilogue, chronicles "all those people [who] lived in spirit in my years of visiting Cape Cod. Their experiences are ones we had in America as we were learning how to be gay. These are the emotions we felt as it was happening."

The adaptation used in this production (by Christie Gesler and H. Richardson Michaels) is serviceable; there are no really major cuts, but the leatherman, Terry, has been written out of the "Franny & her boys" section for reasons I don't quite understand, since the section is devoted to Franny's encouragement of various types of gay men to "take life and change it to what you want it to be," and since leather culture is perhaps the most striking expression of Franny's philosophy.

Franny's speech on leather is also omitted in the play: "You're acting out their dreams and that's what they want to be doing themselves. They want the freedom to look like you look and act like you act.

Maybe a little different, each in his own way. But it's not different from those queens who used to be scared of me. They're jealous in the same way. Envious of you being willing and able to put on clothes that say who you are, or who you want to be, or whatever. Now don't go and get upset at an old queen like me when I say this, but what you got on is drag just as sure as my fanciest ball gown. But that's good. That's being creative and that's making your own way in the world and not letting someone else tell you how you should be…. Wear your leather and show 'em all what a man you are. Show 'em how proud you are of it. It'll do 'em a world of good…."

There's more interplay between the characters in the adaptation than in the novel (which is written as a series of monologues), but I'm not sure if the added theatricality is particularly good for what Preston is trying to express. What was most striking about Franny, the novel, was the way the characters seemed to be speaking through time; the subject was not action, but remembrance.

Meridian is the only theatre group in New York devoted to gay-themed plays. In the past, producers Terry Helbing and Terry Miller have presented Doric Wilson's *Street Theater*, Jane Chamber's *A Late Snow*, and two plays by Robert Chesley – *Stray Dog Story* and *Night Sweat*. The production of *Night Sweat*, that blackest of black comedies, reduced even the most jaded New Yorkers to stuttering outrage; I may have been the only person who saw the play who liked it. (The bio of Chesley in the *Night Sweat* program noted: "Chesley's published work in other media includes … most recently, two ser-monettes disguised as SM porn stories for *Drummer*.")

Franny is a much less radical play than *Night Sweat* (Chesley is by his own admission writing for a gay ghetto audience; Preston isn't), and I can't see any reason why anyone wouldn't enjoy it. It's scheduled for an open-ended run and deserves to be a smash success. You can bring your mother or your lover, or better, both together to it.

John Preston may be the best gay writer in America today. If people won't go to see *Franny*, what will they go to see? You can go to see the tiredest Broadway show and find enough gay people in the audience to fill the tiny Shandol theatre, where *Franny* plays, three or four times over. The gays at one typical performance of *La Cage aux Folles* would be sufficient to keep *Franny* playing to packed houses for weeks.

Time to preach: Gay people have a duty to support works of gay art. Homosexuals fought tooth and nail for decades in order to be able to see good, positive portrayals of gay life on stage and screen. For decades there was absolutely fuckin' nothing on New York stages that addressed gay life. Now, there is Meridian – and the group deserves our support.

Cover art of original Alyson edition

Printed in September 2005
at Gauvin Press Ltd., Gatineau, Québec